THE WEST FAÇADE

THE WEST FAÇADE

Short Stories by
Liz Henderson

Anglepoise
Books

For my family Paul, Laura and Gideon

First published in 2020 by Anglepoise Books

www.oxfordfolio.co.uk

46 Hayfield Road, Oxford OX2 6TU

© Liz Henderson 2020

Design by James Huw King

Cover Illustration by Tessa Powell

ISBN 978-1-9163099-1-3

*

Printed, set and bound by TJ International., Padstow, Cornwall

10 9 8 7 6 5 4 3 2 1

CONTENTS

CREATIVE WRITING COURSE; FIRST TERM*

W^{eek 1} **Openings**

A hand touches my knee as I pull in my chair. He leers. His glasses reflect grey bags under my eyes and an unattractive whiteness about my skin.

Our tutor says. **'Write three sentences to grab the reader's interest,'**

During the night I contemplated ways. Hemlock grew in the fields around our cottage and Fly Agaric was abundant in the woods. Easy to add to a mushroom omelette.

The Groper says nothing when we discuss our work.

More interested in getting his hand into my lap.

Week **2** **Creating Characters**

Sitting next to a student in a black cap, I notice his sharp shoes, buckled with diamanté.

Our tutor says. **'Write about someone you know,'**

Mark walked confidently through life in the knowledge that he was an asset to society; academic, influential, attractive. But his ego was hard to live with.

The Black Cap thinks this male is too stereotypical, not a balanced portrayal.

I glance at his buckles.

Week 3 Settings

I arrive late and take the space near the door, beside a Givenchy handbag. She glances through me as I creep into place.

Our tutor says. **'Take the reader to a familiar place,'**

Morning birds woke me early. The worrying began again. Pink sky showed through the curtain swags. Smells of lavender drifted from the bathroom. I would miss all this if I left. Mark slept beside me, breathing quietly. I could smell his feet.

The Givenchy Bag says she thinks my setting is...'nice', but considers the last sentence to be in poor taste; she looks at my rucksack.

Week 4 Symbolism

An elderly man with a beaky-nose glowers at the table as I take a seat. I stare at his vulture's profile as his long fingers smooth slowly along the black shirt-collar.

Our Tutor says.   **'Create tension using foreshadowing or symbolic imagery,'**

Our first meal together was in his flat. He served me a salad, tight lettuce hearts cut neatly into quarters and drizzled with lemon juice; fennel and mint had been shredded finely and scattered in a circle all round my plate. It was a work of art. An installation.

When we had eaten he gave me a gold chain, not real gold; we were students. He put it round my neck and closed the clasp. For a moment he rested his hands on my bare shoulders. I remember how cold his hands were.

Beaky-Nose is complimentary, but disregards my insistence that this really was the first meal that Mark ever served me. He says my writing makes him dread what is coming next.

He's odd. What's he on about?

Week 5 Sex

A neat grey smile and a suit straight from work, greet me. He stretches his legs under the table as I approach, winks and strokes his chin. My neck sweats.

Our Tutor says. **'Avoid cliché and slush,'**

Sex? What sex? We never have been good. He used to fumble, refusing to let me help him. It broke any rhythm and desire. God only knows how I managed to get pregnant - sex hadn't featured since my termination. Mark would have been a good dad.

The Grey Smile writes one sentence; a question. I pass it straight back to him ... how disgusting!

Our Tutor sees me blushing and abruptly brings the session to an end.

Week 6 Getting Ideas

Shopping spills at the young mother's feet. Her gypsy scarf is tight to her face. She is sparkly keen.

Our Tutor says, **'Photos, maps, smells, objects, memories, sounds, observations, headlines, jokes, characters, experiences... open your imagination. Ideas come from everywhere,'**

I had a penknife on my key ring. A present from Dad when I was only eight. It said he trusted me, believed in me and made me know myself. I was disciplined and strong, could do anything; make a success of whatever I did. Where was that feeling now? But I still had the weapon.

Gypsy Scarf grabs at her phone... She'll have to go. ... Husband. At home. The baby!

Week 7   Dialogue

A chair is empty beside an elderly feather-and-fan sweater. I ask permission join her. Tired eyes flick over my face as I gesture to the chair. She shrugs.

Our tutor says. **'Make this exchange real and convincing,'**

'Can't you see, for God's sake? You're so fucking selfish, Mark. What About me?'

'Don't resort to swearing, let's have a reasoned discussion.'

'Fuck 'reasoned' anything. It's my life you're wrecking'.

'Listen. I earn good money to support you, work long hours to achieve a respected position.'

'Exactly. You have a sodding life, but think about me for once.'

'Come on. Let's talk about it darling.'

Feather-and-Fan draws in her lips and remains silent. The language offends, I fear.

Week 8   Time Shifts

The woman in a loud orange T-shirt finishes her doughnut.

Our tutor says. **'Watch your tenses,'**

I remembered a day of punting. He had completed his exams and was relaxed and funny. White wine, strawberries and a rug on the grass. Love was in his grey eyes.

How did things go so wrong? We no longer touch. Together we are critical and abrasive. I could imagine myself happier with someone else.

The Orange T-shirt turns to me. Her wet eyes search my face. She squeezes my hand and looks ... heartfelt. She asks me to reconsider. Nothing is worse than being alone.

I remind her that this is a creative writing course.

* Winner of the OUDCE International Short Story Competition 2010.

LAGUNA

D eep white sinks, pipes curved, fossilized serpents in the wash-house. Overhead drying sheets shifted in the midday heat. The House-Boy had found an old Primus stove and showed the children how it worked. Kate was ten now; old enough to be able to use it, he said. Hong Kong had few toy shops. Their only supplies came rarely; from America.

Crouching on the stone floor the two girls could cook for their old bears, who sat and gazed at the blue flames with their glass eyes.

'You're only five Emma, it's dangerous. I'll pour in the meths,' Kate said as she placed a tiny funnel into the tray.

'I'll strike the match then.'

'No you're not allowed. If Mother found out...'

But snatching up the matches Emma struck one.

'Don't! You're not allowed. You're too little.'

'Shut up. I don't have to do what you say.'

Emma held the lighted match to the tray, an almost invisible blue flame flickered. They waited. A mingled smell of newly struck match and hot metal rose. The girls hunkered down, skirts tucked into knickers. Emma placed a small tin of water onto the supporting frame of the stove. Kate pumped the tiny lever and an invisible spray of paraffin ignited into a yellow and blue jet. The tin on the stove still showed the writing, 'powered milk', but then, as they watched, the letters curled and blackened, peeling off to reveal gun-metal tin.

'The tin's getting too hot.'

'I know,' Kate said. She shuffled back from the heat. 'The water's nearly boiling. It's never done that so fast before.' The bubbling water in the little milk-tin, began to spit. But there was no handle.

'The fire's too fierce. Get back.' She kicked the tin off the hob, into the drain beside them. It clattered into a pool of soapy water. Small clouds of steam rose, into the sheets hanging above.

'Why was it so hot?'

'Don't know, maybe I pumped it too hard. I'll have to turn it off or...'

She took a handful of her skirt as protection and grabbed the little tap in the base. Starting back from the heat she'd moved too quickly. A plume of yellow flames leaped across the stone floor as the stove tipped. Little shins grazed the duck-boards. They both screamed and fell to the floor.

The flames settled and died, leaving an acrid smell. Both children ran to squeeze under the veranda.

≈

Their Amah mistook bruises for dirt at bath time. She scrubbed at them to get them clean.

'Where's Mother gone?' Emma asked. And again, at bedtime, 'Where *is* she?'

'Missy on ferry to mainland.'

'Perhaps she's heard that Daddy's ship's in,' Emma said, 'I don't think he's coming back though is he?' Kate did not answer. 'What will happen to us without him?'

≈

Lunch was on the veranda in the shade the next day. Amah stood beside them policing table manners and folding the dry washing into a deep basket.

'Where is mother ... I keep asking you?' Emma insisted.

'Busy shopping,'

'I don't believe you. She was crying again last night.

'No crying.'

'Liar!' Emma shouted.

'Emma!' Kate said, 'don't be rude. Say sorry to Amah.'

'I heard Mother crying in the night. It makes me cry too.'

Kate took her hand under the table and gave it a squeeze.

≈

In their beds after lunch, they watched the mosquito nets above them wafting in the draught of the fan. Slowly they drifted into sleep. Kate dreamed of her father, bringing presents; a real monkey, a diamond ring. Emma woke up and lay looking at the small photo of him beside her bed. She remembered his writing on the back, she knew what it said, 'To my naughty monkey. I will love you for ever and ever.'

She lay picturing her mother returning with a tricycle; a Meccano set or ... best of all a beautiful doll, with eyes that blinked and clothes for special occasions. One of Emma's friends had received a long box from America for her birthday. Nestling in powder-blue paper was a doll. Her friend lifted it out to show them how it could stand.

'Look,' she said, 'she can walk too,' and she held the doll's hand, rocking it slowly so it strode beside her. More like a miniature friend than a doll. 'Josie' came with a complete wardrobe. She could get married in the finest brocade, go skating with real skates on her feet, ride in her jodhpurs, sunbathe in her sundress and go to school in her uniform. Her ball-gown was covered in purple sequins and had tiny silk-covered buttons from neck to waist.

≈

In the morning their Mother was back, but she had gone again before they could see her.

'She could have stayed for breakfast with us.'

'Maybe she's had some news,' Kate said. 'Stop pouting Emma.'

Amah stood in the shade. The morning was hot, a small breeze blew from the sea. They could hear shouts of the sampan-dwellers as they dipped and twisted their yulohs across the harbour below. The long needles of the Casuarina tree whispered, the children ate in silence. They followed Amah to the wash-house and listened, looking at each other and giggling while she grumbled about the naughty mess. She shook her finger at them.

'You not be naughty now; you be good girls like before.' The sheets had to be washed again. She moaned, in her pidgin talk and made them turn the handle of the mangle for her. But Mother never knew.

≈

Later in the day, Kate brushed the veranda tiles with her hands, before opening a tin of marbles.

'You know, when Mother just sits and won't talk to us? I think she's fallen asleep with her eyes open when she's like that.' Emma whispered.

'I know ... something important must have happened.'

'What kind of important?'

'News of where Daddy is, or wondering if he has been taken prisoner, or bad news about the war. It could be anything. Anyway... let's have a game of marbles.'

'I don't want to. They always roll off the step into the grass and get lost. It's boring. I'm going to see what Amah's doing.'

≈

The drawing-room was covered with piles of table-cloths and mats, bundles of napkins and lace doylies. Kate wandered off to her room to read. Emma lay on her back on the rattan matting by the garden doors, peering along the silver-green nap of the carpet through the legs of the chairs and tables.

She could see the stout legs of the camphor-wood chest. What was in there? Opening the lid, she breathed in its medicinal smell. It reminded her of Mother, of this house, of family times round the table, Christmas and birthdays.

The chest was almost empty, except for a roll of old sheeting and some tissue paper. Emma lifted it out. Inside was a silk evening-gown that smelt of Mother's perfume.

She had once lifted the ground glass lid of the scent bottle on her mother's dressing-table. The bottle was a glass lady, tall and thin. She was wearing a gown like this one in the chest. She stretched her arms above her head, her face tipped back and her long glass hair hung down her naked back. She stood on a plinth on which was written a word in black, '*Indiscreet*'.

Emma liked the sound of that name; 'indiscreet, indiscreet'. Then she remembered where she had heard it before. At the Country Club one of her mother's friends had said it. They had been talking in whispers about Mother's new boyfriend. They had stopped when they saw her listening.

The white dress trailed against Emma's body, sweeping the floor as she turned and spun. In the window's reflection she knew she had seen it before; in the photo on the piano. It was Mother's wedding dress. Draping it over the settee she went to find Kate, but she stopped to look into the chest with its heavy lid propped open. She noticed the russet wood inside and leant in to feel it. Her nostrils filled with its magic smell. She climbed into the chest and sat down with her hands on the webbing straps that held the lid. Without warning the lid tipped and bumped down on her head.

Plunged immediately into darkness, surrounded by the

intense smell and deadened silence, at first it felt a special place, exciting. But when she braced herself against the lid, pushing with all her strength, she realised she was trapped. The great brass lock must have fallen and caught.

The camphor's perfume was now overwhelming; sickening. Without a chink of light her prison was small, constricting and baffling as she shouted. She gulped in that once-treasured scent in gasps, sobbing and beating her fists on the floor and sides of the chest.

She knew Amah would assume she was with Kate. She would not search for her until tea time. The drawing-room was not a place they were allowed to play. No one would look there. Suddenly a small light in the darkness made her jump; the luminous dial of her watch. With her wrist to her face she watched the long hand creep from the twelve to the one; then after a long time, to the two.

She cried, shouting until she was hoarse.

Kate had read her a story about a boy who, lost and alone in the jungle, sang to keep himself brave. She hummed quietly, nursery rhymes and carols; then songs from her Christmas book. When they ran out she improvised with tunes that rambled and wavered; a whispered chanting of words, repeated over and over. Later a strange dream about Father coming home to find her; dead, locked in the chest. She searched for her hanky to wipe her eyes; sweating face and neck.

Mother would not come back in time. She continued to kick and pummel and shout. She felt she was disappearing into the distance, her voice fading. She thought of Mother, high heels clicking, and straight black stocking seams under her swaying frock. Mother was not there to hear her shouts. She thought of her walking ahead of her, hand in hand with...was it father or one of her boyfriends? She heard him whisper 'Indiscreet Darling'. They giggled.

Emma drifted away.

It was Mother's voice calling her name that woke her. She beat on the lid with her fists. She screamed until her ears hurt. Then the lid opened onto the blinding brightness of afternoon.

'Emma darling, thank God. Thank God. How did you get in there? What on earth were you doing? We thought you had run away.' She lay still on her mother's lap, calmed by the soft stroking touch and familiar smell of perfume and cigarettes.

'Now then my naughty Emma, we've told you before. You are not allowed in the drawing-room. Promise me that you won't play in here again... please.'

Emma lay back to look up into her face.

'I thought I'd never be found. I shouted and shouted. I thought I was going to die!'

Her mother held her, rocked her and hummed a little song Emma had learned at Nursery school. There was a close spell of silence. Emma stopped crying.

Slowly she pulled herself away from the embrace.

'But I found your wedding dress Mother.' Jumping up, she picked up the dress and held it in front of her. Her mother gasped, hands over her mouth and sat silently, crying. Emma tried to hug her lap to comfort and stroke her. Kate came running in.

'Kate darling, I was hoping to bring home such a surprise.' Her lace hanky twisted in her hands. Kate stood beside them.

'I'm so disappointed.'

'What were you going to bring home?' Kate asked.

'It was going to be ... a present ... a *wonderful* surprise ... for you both. I saw the merchant ship in the harbour. That's why I took the early ferry.'

She wrung her hands and, wiping her forehead, she went to her bedroom where they could hear her crying.

It would have been nice to have had a story at bedtime, but they could hear her playing Chopin downstairs. Again they lay watching the mosquito nets swaying in the rhythmic draughts of the fan.

Emma whispered, 'Daddy used to like her playing like this. Tell me something about him, Kate. I've nearly forgotten what he's like.'

'He's really clever; has such good ideas, that's why he's an engineer here. Hong Kong needs electricity and he designs the pumps for Hydro-electric power stations. Do you remember when I asked him about rainbows? He took us into his den and he showed us sunlight on a prism, the colours so brilliant and clear.'

Emma climbed under Kate's net. They lay, forbidden and curled-up together, whispering. Kate put her arms round Emma; breathing into her ear. 'Anything might happen. We may have to be very brave Emma, but I will always look after you. We'll stick together and look after each other.'

'And we'll always remember him', Emma said.

≈

Next day they sat on the swings by the Casuarina tree, keeping their bare feet away from the little cones that lay waiting for tender soles. The air was still and sticky. The movement of the swings lifted the hems of their skirts from damp legs. They heard the car on the drive and jumped down to run to meet her. She too was running, smiling, laughing and calling their names. She put down her bags on the lawn and crouched to embrace them, one in each arm.

'I had another phone call – it was exactly what I had longed for - I went back again and again – but they kept telling me they hadn't arrived yet... but today it happened. I'm so excited. Fabulous news.'

As they untied the string on the parcels, she smiled into their faces. Kate glanced back at the car. It was empty; no passenger.

They unwrapped the tissue paper in the boxes; but before they uncovered the contents, they both knew. Two beautiful dolls, each with a suitcase full of clothes.

Emma tenderly cradled her doll, rocking it gently in her arms.

Kate stared at her box and hung her head.

~

Mother sat with them for lunch, chatting on about her rush to the shop when she'd heard the dolls had come in. Many other mothers had been disappointed. Eventually she sat back in her chair to look at the dolls' clothes spread on the table.

'Isn't that *just* what you both wanted most of all?' and she sighed, 'At last!'

'She's lovely,' Emma said as she stroked the too-shiny hair. I'm going to call her 'Indiscreet' ... I love that name.' Mother smiled. 'I'll call her 'Indie' for short.'

'What's yours going to be called Kate?' Mother asked.

'I don't really ...' Kate looked into her lap. 'I had hoped...'

'What?' Mother said, 'What had you hoped Kate darling? Do you think you are too old for a doll then?'

'No. It's not that. It's just that ... well,' her lips quivered, 'the thing I wanted most of all ... well... what I really hoped you were bringing me was ...'

'What is all this?' Mother looked dismayed. 'I have been rushing about doing my best to get you a lovely doll to play with and you're going to tell me you didn't really want it.'

'I wanted ... I thought you were going to the mainland because you'd heard ... we thought...' Kate stood up and ran off.

'Oh God,' Mother sighed, 'I was just trying to ...' She quickly stood up and left the room, hanky pressed to her face. Emma sat at the table with Indie beside her. Only the cicadas in the garden and some distant noises from the kitchen disturbed the quiet. She picked

Indie up, rested her on the table, slowly brushed her hair and sang her name over and over.

≈

Kate was having her piano lesson. Emma took Indie to the top veranda. The breeze blew off the sea in the afternoons. Indie would enjoy it there. Her Mother was lying on her bed as she crept past her open door. She saw Emma and called to her.

'We mustn't cry Emma; there's nothing we can do to make him come back. We just have to remember how much he loved us all, what a dear and wonderful person .... we must just keep going and hope that he's all right.'

'But what if he's not?'

'It's best not to think of it... just look forward to the future together.'

'I don't think I can even remember what he looks like. Mumma. Where's his photo gone? It used to be here on the table.

'It is here still, in the drawer, but it is too formal,' she said as she passed the photo of father sitting behind his desk. 'This one is my favourite one'. And there he was; handsome in dinner jacket and black bow tie. Her head tipped back as they danced, he gazed adoringly at her. Emma hardly knew him.

They lay for a while remembering picnics and beach parties. But Emma could not really remember without her Mother's prompting.

The phone rang.

'Very well. I'll come straight away. Thank you for letting me know. Should I bring my overnight things? Yes. Yes of course. Goodbye.'

'I have to go Emma. Please just stay out of trouble while I'm gone. Go and find Kate.' She called as she ran into her dressing room, 'And no getting into chests young lady.'

≈

Kate had homework to do after tea. Emma went back upstairs into her Mother's room. Taking the photo and holding it close to her face, she searched for clues that would make her remember. She wanted to hear his voice, see how he walked and moved.

Searching through his suits, shirts and jackets helped. She began to remember him, setting out for work each day; his soapy smell. She found his brief-case and rummaged through a few papers. Right at the bottom there was a white envelope with photos inside it. Her mother in a smart tailored costume, Granny and Grandpa when they were younger standing by a funny old pram; Benjie, their Labrador. She only just remembered having to leave him behind. The last photo was smaller than the rest. There she was shouting with laughter; a very dirty summer dress, two saucepan-lids covered in mud. Emma could almost hear the racket. On the back father had written, 'My precious, naughty monkey.'

She took it to bed with her that night. 'I am his naughty-monkey', she whispered and lay very still in the heat. It was hard to breathe, she needed the cool night-air. Kate was asleep so she crept out onto the veranda. It was cooler out there but she knew the mosquitoes would be biting.

Her Mother had not returned. Now what was she doing ... not buying a doll in the middle of the night? She crept along to her mother's room when she noticed the black ladder fixed to the wall. It led to the flat roof above. Forbidden territory.

Hanging onto each rung carefully she climbed up into the night breeze; stared down at a chaos of twinkling lights. Resting her chin on her arms on the railing. The lights below marked out the streets. Just car horns or a dog disturbed the night. She tried to trace the roads she knew; to Kate's school, the market and ferry terminal. Only then did she notice the enormous black shape slipping towards the docks. Its lights gliding slowly against those of the town. Tiny black tugs pulling and shunting. A liner.

'Kate! Kate!' she screamed. Kate came running, scolding and threatening. She climbed the ladder, shouting loudly, threatening to tell Mother. 'Naughty GIRL!'

From the top rung she saw the ship. They held each other and dared not speak. Watching, swatting the mosquitoes, waiting.

The phone rang downstairs. Armah, could not find them. Terrified, she was shrieking their names,

'Missie Kate! Missie Emma!' Get dressed quick.'

OUR BOY

He'd been missing for three hours.

The house, shed and garden; we searched.

Local Police searched; hills, rivers; with dogs.

Everywhere, over and over. The garage, garden, playroom, loft.

Our family was used to it but his 'volcanoes' are more frequent ... a new school loomed.

This was his longest absence. He had gone from us... suddenly not there... again and again... ever since he had learned to walk.

Withdrawals, rages, upsets, furies. He was nine. We all knew his hiding places; the 'escapes' as he called them. The shed, the room behind the garage, the car floor splaces, under the Land Rover, crouching in his willow-hut, or in the greenhouse. We had put an old armchair in the rabbit's shed ... He whispered into the long ears. They were a comfort to each other; he was not there.

His little brother tried the shed door again. It had been locked. He pushed and heaved, shouted his name and ran to the house to tell.

'And there's a funny smell too'.

The small window showed only grime and cobwebs. Inside was dark. There was a terrible smell leaking out of the crack under the door.

All three of us mustered ideas to help us to get him out; screwdrivers, hack–saws, wafer biscuits, lemonade, jam sandwiches, a mallet, chisels, his little stool, a torch, joss–sticks and matches.

Each of us tried.

≈

'If you get in here', he shouted, 'I've got a steak knife from the kitchen ... 'GO AWAY!!' There was an enraged, scrambled screaming noise from the back of his throat.

Bribes and offers of rewards intensified his threats.

We both waited taking it in turns. I whispered to him ... told him we were glad he'd found a safe place to hide... silence. Mike said he could stay there as long as he liked, but he mustn't do anything that would hurt him. I reassured him that when he came out he could choose what he wanted for supper. I whispered that it would be getting dark soon. Would he like a torch? He could have a torch if he promised to stay safe.

We took it in turns to keep watch outside.

He hummed on every breath.

I sat with my back to the door ... listening to his drone ... not a tune or a regular rhythm ... monotonous meandering humming ...on in-breaths and out-breaths. The floor creaked. He was moving about. I could hear him mumbling to himself ... there were no recognisable words.

All his movements stopped. I imagined him sitting on the floor rocking and rocking; rocking and rocking, as he so often did. With my ear against the key hole, his sounds had no form; they still came but they were internalised... far down in the back of his throat, quiet, uncertain. A fluctuating gravelly chant ... for comfort ... I knew.

Night had come slowly. We crept with torches, listened at the door. Silence now. We knew he was in there. It was dark ... he feared the dark. After a few seconds we heard him droning again.

Mike shone the torch through the window... talked to him quietly.

We heard the key turn.

We blocked the doorway expecting him to barge and run.

Slowly he stepped out onto the step, into the night; hair tousled; face tired; white, looking dazed, staring at the ground.

No eye contact. Never any eye contact.

We coaxed him into the kitchen; sat watching him eat; his usual choice; macaroni cheese. The only thing he'd eat. Cramming handfuls into his mouth with his big spoon.

Silence but for his stertorous chewing.

Later we put on his favourite CD…and his brother started the disco-ball rotating. We all stared at the psychedelic colours that streamed above the chimney breast and round the sitting-room; flashing to the frequencies of the Gregorian chants. Eventually he lay on his back on the hearth rug. Eyes open, utterly still.

The boys went up to bed together with no fuss.

No-one spoke. It was best that way. He didn't like being 'tucked in'.

≈

When all was quiet we went with a torch to the shed; wanting to find the source of the sickening stench.

Inside, an area of the floor, a metre square, had been marked out with a pattern of bleached twigs, set together in crosses. Inside this small arena was a body. The remains of a rat.

We crouched, covering our noses. The furry head had whiskers, long yellow teeth, empty eye sockets. Radiating around the head, were golden petals from the sunflowers in his garden.

An early Russian icon!

Beneath the head lay the small body, incised from neck to tail. A short stick wedged open the abdominal cavity. Inside, the bloody remains of entrails. The tiny heart had been cut out and was resting beside the body on a dried leaf. The bones of the front and back legs had been roughly cleaned of all flesh. Fore-legs spread wide and weighted with stones.

What was it, this Christ-on-the-cross image? The rat's tail rested between its legs, like a stake to which the body would have been fixed.

Mike took photos of it with his phone. Could be useful at tomorrow's appointment. But for now the decision.

To leave it would imply approval; approbation even. To clear it away would be to engage his overwhelming rage the next morning. We had to take him for his appointment. We left it and locked the shed.

I could not sleep.

LUXEMBOURG GARDENS, PARIS:
SIDONIE AND PASCAL

SIDONIE

Gusts tip the small model-boats' sails, acute angles to the water. Capsize imminent! Number seventeen, close to the wind, wobbles, takes the lead. Children run round the raised pond chanting, 'dix-sept, dix-sept'. A small boy beside me rises to his toes. 'Allez six' he whispers, clapping hands, anticipating his triumph. Too soon. Number six slams down on a gust, just short of the final mark. Cheering, the others lift their winner into the air.

Dust marks my sandaled feet. I look at the many chairs. Once painted green, now faded, scuffed to gunmetal. Metal chairs in scattered groups round the pond and beside the paths. But few are right for me. The reclining ones are essential today. There must be one that allows the sitter to lie back, tilted at 45°; one of 'My' chairs. Just one, vacant for me to lie in. To doze. I need to tip my head to the sun, lie back and rest. The sun is warm. Parisians are here; out of their boxes into the summer air. I examine a chipped finger-nail, flick ash from my skirt. There's a gardener nearby, clipping. He's watching me.

The right chair. A reclining chair. Come ON! They cannot all be taken.

A young man pauses, turns to look at me and smiles.

'Might see you later' in his glance. I turn away to catch the chat and whisper of passers-by but know he is watching my bare legs... Nice.

Concentrate... find it! The right chair. Keep walking. Focus. It has to be spotted and claimed in seconds.

I scan for that superior kind of chair. One that permits the sitter to repose in comfort, a tilted sturdy support. I search out some steps, a clear viewpoint. My surveillance system sweeps; radar scanning for body positions. That tilt of 45°degrees to horizontal. I watch for it to flash onto my screen. Searching. Searching.

A gardener stands to stretch his back. I catch his eye. He knows the game.

'Come on Sidonie!' I whisper. 'There must be one.'

Some movement not far from me. An elderly man struggles to sit upright, pulling on the metal arms. He rubs his face and stretches, stays upright to stare at the children. He is coming round, recovering, red-faced from sleep. The yacht-race takes his attention. He collects his bags. I walk nearer. Just an amble or others might see my intention.

A blonde girl near me threatens my position. Her watch on him is less subtle, almost a stare. She will not notice if I keep moving. I turn to let the breeze take hair from my face. She looks past our shared locus at the tangle of chairs and people around her, at children and their model boats. Then a furtive glance in my direction. She knows.

A tactical fight for supremacy has begun. The final stages of the contest are unfolding. The end game is coming. I have the king and two knights, but she is approaching with her queen. Survival of the fittest. GO for it Sidonie. I take a step towards the old man. His hands clasp the seat. He rocks to and fro, pushing his weight onto the edge and, heaving, he unfurls. His grasp leaves the chair-back.

I sprint forward dodging chairs, shoes, bags and cases that lie in my way. I am fleet. This chair will be mine. I am quick to dodge. Eyes fixed on the prey. The girl, blunders, approaches; lurching, clumsy. I run the last steps, reaching out to touch first. To win the race.

'Excusez-moi', I say smiling as her hand contacts a moment after mine. Handbag on my lap, I slip down, head back, facing the sun. A long sigh. She is beside me. Aggrieved. Shading my eyes I try to smile.

'Desolée.' I say with a shrug. She stands; as she was the moment my hand touched the prize. Curling fair hair frames her face. Blue eyes gaze into mine. Disappointment? Rage? Oh for god's sake. Get over it. It was a fair game. I WON!

My breathing slows. I glance at my watch. Fifty precious minutes to myself. I keep my eyes shut but I wonder what is she doing? I envisage her still standing too close. She staring; resentful. Are witnesses pointing me out, the 'glorious victor'? With an arm to shade my face I see she has turned to walk away and is watching the model boats. She's leaning on the railings round the pond beside me. Her cotton jacket, fitted and floral, a little passé. Smart though. The red bag she has on her shoulder has hitched up one side of her long skirt. I look for bare brown legs and trim red heels. I know they will match her bag and the petals on her jacket.

But her legs are not brown, and no chic shoes. They do not match anything. Below her lifted hem are metal callipers and a boot at an awkward angle.

She turns and sees me looking.

I lean back into the chair with a long sigh.

PASCAL

I must have been a dog once, an ordinary mutt, a mongrel for certain. My Ma wanted her boy to be a greyhound, a playful Labrador, or a Great Dane. Not an Alsatian with brains or a sniffing Spaniel.

I don't linger at tasty smells on bushes, but I know what it feels like. I went on a date a few years ago. She kissed me at her gate. I'm still on that extended lead, stretching my neck to smell her again. There is something about the way a dog resists the restraint of a lead, continues to sniff the draft of her passing. I can identify with that. I can smell and taste her still and when I see some of these girls in the park, I'm like a dog on a lead.

Longing to linger over their scent.

It was always the same. 'Never mind Pascal; you'll just try harder next time won't you?' Every Sports Day my mother would say. 'You CAN be a winner. I want you to WIN. Try harder next time like the other boys do. Do it for me son eh? Make me proud of you! On the beach it was... 'Go Pascal! Use both hands. Get the ball, jump higher!' My friends would run off into the sea with girls. I'd watch their long tanned legs, the splashing and shrieking and the fondling hands.

In Paris I escaped from her criticism. We don't keep in touch.

At first I couldn't find a job. 'No fixed address', so I was forced to doss in the streets. One evening I kicked away rubbish under the bridge by Notre Dame, making a space to sit. The floodlit towers reflected in the river. I liked the look of this place for my sleeping bag. Majesty, history and grace in prospect all night. There was a rolled up towel that was heavy enough for me to know there was something inside it. As I pulled at the corner of it a small puppy fell out; thin, cold and hungry. I called him Cloche. Short for 'clochard'; a tramp. I gave him milk and food. We survived together under the bridge for many nights.

He followed me to Employment Offices, waited outside. When the job in the Luxembourg Gardens was offered, I knew it would suit me. I had helped at home in the garden; knew one flower from another. But 'Chiens interdits' on signs, in the flower beds and pathways. It was made clear at interview. Little Cloche, skinny and smooth, his stumpy legs whizzing 'wind-ups' under him. His tight white tail stuck up as he ran, a metronome, marking time for his feet. What would I do with him all day if he was not allowed into the Park?

I stopped at the gate on the first morning, pointed to the gates and said 'Non' very firmly a few times. He listened to me, head on one side. I had never spoken to him in that voice. When I took off his lead he seemed to know. So from that day, he goes where he likes; to the bins at the best restaurants I guess, from the garlic on his breath when he returns.

I have loved the flower-beds that begin in spring with stitched lines of tiny plants. A flat tapestry whose rhythmic sewing is rooted in the earth, serried, measured and formal. I enjoy watching them through the summer as they jumble into a psychedelic mass of clashing brilliance. It is rewarding working on the flowers and pollards, large raised pond and wide paths creating a grand foreground for the imposing neo-classical palace. I am happy with this work; digging the soil, watching life in the park. Each passer-by conjures a story and all this inspired me to try my hand at writing.

I really may have been a dog. Reincarnated? I will go out of my way to please people I meet, especially if I get to know them. I'd like to meet a girl, a kind one. We could walk together and we might fall in love. I could look after her; treasure her, and she might come to respect and love me, too. I do like the odd pat on the back of course, I don't wag my tail or lick at hands... but I do sometimes piss in the bushes.

I have my own place now. I've begun writing a collection of stories, about the park and the people. I watch the visitors passing. Lovers with lips and tongues too public. Automaton mothers rocking prams. Young men 'eyeing' short skirts. Old people 'zimmering'. Children hot and pouty. Priests striding with brief cases. Toddlers falling on their nappied arses.

Towards the end of each day Cloche is there, by the park gate, tail up, wagging and waiting. We walk home in silence. He understands. He is tired too. We reach the top floor, both out of breath from the stairs. I unlock the door to my attic, but I have learned to stand back. Cloche has to be first to enter. He is the master here. I stand on my bed to open the window. It gives a glimpse of the sky and the distant inclined slate of the Palace roofs. Pigeons nest in the gutters nearby; their cooing is a soothing presence.

I sit with a glass of cheap wine and read my work aloud to Cloche, each evening. I can hear how strong my voice becomes; different. He looks into my eyes, twisting his head, watching, hoping I think, that he might hear a word he knows, 'squirrel' or 'walk'. After supper I settle to writing. Sometimes it gets to me. I can get emotional. Cloche comes to lick my face and hands. He whimpers. He can't cry, so how can he sympathise with me? He lies on his back, legs splayed in the air, waiting for my foot to rub in some reassurance.

Each day there's a story I can tell of the Luxembourg Gardens. Today there was disabled girl I've seen before. She missed her chance to get a reclining chair. I could see she needed to rest in the sun. Empty inclined chairs are rare on sunny days. She leaned against the balustrade by the pond. She saw me watching. I raised both my hands with disappointment. 'Tant pis', I whispered and she laughed. She stood for a long time, watching the children with their little sticks guiding the dinghies. Finally she turned away from their shrieks and banter. She was clumsy; limping towards the park-gate. As she closed it behind her she looked back at me and smiled. She knew I was watching her.

I've put one of those chairs behind the shed now. When I see her coming tomorrow I'll set it out for her and watch her lie back.

She will smile at me again and I'll wag my tail.

FAREWELL MARTY

Although you're dead Marty, it's well weird here at your funeral. I feel kinda feel like you're with me, waiting for the hearse. It's coming, creeping in the chapel gates; black stretch–limo... small crowd watching. Grey face behind the wheel; he's a top–hat solemn git all–right. I'm standing 'ere, beside the group of mourners. There's the Weepers and Silent Ones and them's that can't stop talking. You know what mate? ... something fishy's going on 'ere. I'm trying not to laugh. It's not I'm not sad; just none of it seems... well... real.

We're all seated now. Chapel's packed. Nice your family's all 'ere, and there's also what looks like West End spivs; art dealers are they? There's a few mates too... ex–cons I suppose.

Your mum must of chose the music; Judy Garland's 'Somewhere Over the Rainbow'. I can kinda see you over the church, floating up in the rain, 'way up high'.

The coffin's coming... passing me now. It's one of them wicker ones...all covered with football rosettes an'at. It creaks as it goes by, and you dead inside... talk about 'embarrassing bodies' eh?

Ah... the sun's just come out... stained-glass is turning us all into multi-coloured ghosts. Is that your doing? Are you turning on 'special effects'? Is it you... un–dead hovering over us? I still feel you're 'ere... can almost 'ear you singing along with Vera Lynn... and your dirty laugh an'all.

Funny! I've just noticed that the bearers' faces ... all sweaty. Under their tight black clothes are bulging muscles. They're struggling to carry you. Why's that I wonder? When I saw you last week you looked even thinner than ever... months of prison food... eh? I thought you might be ill or somefing.

Everyfing's gone quiet now. You'd be well touched by all this; the atmosphere. But knowing you as I do, you'd not be reverent. Neither of us could ever stand pompous chapel-crap like this. I know what we'd do if you were sitting here beside me. We'd be clearing our throats, or sharing a quiet fart with the rest of 'em. This silence is embarrassing. The mourners are like a bloody 'audience'. It's like some kind of performance; an 'installation' in those Tate Modern Tanks, graffiti on the walls, oil drums banging. I'm waiting for skateboarders to fly in and see clouds of coloured smoke.

Now there's a too-long silence while the vicar's shoes squeak up the steps to the pulpit. He stands with his hands resting on the rail, arms out straight. Here comes the eulogy.

'Marty's Mum told me that he was a good and loving little boy, how he loved to help her in the kitchen.

He was her oldest child and so treasured for that'

Blimey! This guy needs no mic. His booming bloody voice! Are they born with vocal chords that lead them into the church? You'll never guess what though. Your brother's nodding his head. Yes? LOVING? He's still wearing his hair over his ears. D'you remember your tendency to bite? It deprived him of the luxury of two ears for the rest of his life. He must be wearing contact lenses now coz he ain't in them lop-sided specs he wore all through school. You never told me what in Christ's name you were doing? He was three years old, poor little git!

'Marty was the centre of a big loving family. He was always there for any of them when they were unhappy.'

The vicar's voice don't get no better. I want to jump up and shout, 'not when I was his best mate at school 'e kicked Gracey out the 'ouse and she slept in our shed. Not when 'e was banged up at eighteen, and then again at twenty six, thirty three and finally two years ago, at forty.'

But I'm not going to spoil this moment. I'm watching your Tania and Gran, hankies to their eyes, listening to this fairy tale. Tania's taken your Gran's arm. They share a smile. Your Gran's quite deaf now. 'Shame Grandad's not here eh?' She shouts. 'He loved our Smarty.' She says – too loud.

'He worked hard and did well at school'.

Oh yeah right. What's he know? When, and if, you went to school, you were a lazy, distracting bastard, out to make us all laugh and jeering at any of us who worked. The vicar looks over heads to the back of the church where your dad lifts his drunken head from his chest. His eyes search the vaulted ceiling; trying to remember his son? But he'd have no memory of your childhood; in the nick as he was through your youth.

'He was a successful business man.'

Smiles and nods all round. Yeah. Well. If bankrupt twice and sometime millionaire counts... but I'm not letting you off what you owe me, total about three K, I reckon. My digs always a refuge, and me waiting at the nick gates whenever you were released? Friend or not I want paying back, you shit.

'Happy Marriage.'

The vicar is tipping his head to one side to give a smile directly to Tania; fishnets, platform 'eels and a black fascinator; keeping her end up as usual. I guess she'll not be alone for long, probably glad to be rid of you.

'Lovely dad to his kids.'

Poor little Katie can't lift her head... just shaking with sobs, hand on her bump but no bloke there with her. And she still at school. She's better than all of you put together. D'you know what? She deserved a better dad, someone who was at home of a night to help with her homework perhaps. A role model. Naa.... . Now I think about it. There was none of that in your toolbox... you couldn't of done it, even if you'd been around.

Gracey is leaning over and puts a loving arm round Katie's shoulders. She's a lovely creature, can't be your genes though.

'It was shocking and sadly unexpected death so young.'

The thing is Marty, I know you too well. This death – somehow don't seem right. I reckon your plans must of gone wrong. Yeah. Perhaps you were trying a 'get-away', to hide in some foreign haven where you could spend your haul for the rest of your life. But would you really have been in a speedboat? You couldn't swim. The paper said that witnesses saw the sharks, but no-one came forward to say they saw you being mauled an'at. No-one dragged your mutilated body to the beach. It all seemed... well a bit 'fishy' ...'scuse the pun eh? I can tell you that the pewful of suits at the back are not amused; shades, sharp jackets and tight lips and a look of fury on their faces ... well pissed off. How much did you owe them I wonder?

'Ashes to ashes, dust to dust.'

I reckon that's all they are here to see.

Hymn 'Fight the Good Fight'.

What a choice! Not that you were actually any good at boxing, but if life is a contest you certainly played it with gusto mate... but there were victims of your crimes. Like poor Auntie May, hiding in the dark in her bed while you ransacked her living room for cash to feed your 'abit. So not actually a 'good fight' I'd say.

We're all standing to sing. The bruisers at the back are silent, I notice... mouths shut tight, except a little chap, could be Welsh. His singing came from deep in his little barrel-chest. 'Chrrrist be thy strength and Chrrrist thy right, Lay hold on life and it shall be....' his voice is soaring above all others.

Now the church is quiet and we're sat down again. Your Gran's just proclaimed,

'Marty's friends at the back gave that some welly. Nice of them all to come!'

After the blessing it is Vera Lynn

> *'We'll Meet Again,*
> *Don't know where,*
> *Don't know when,*
> *But I know we'll meet again some sunny day.'*

Is your mum religious or does she, like me, suspect somefing's up? I wonder.

It's raining now and bleedin' cold. We're at the graveside and your coffin is being lowered; your mum and Katie throw in plastic roses and step back, grabbing hold of each other. One whispers your name, the other rests a hand on her bump. 'Ashes to ashes' an'at.

I'll stay here until mine is the only car left in the car park, just to make sure it is all done; finished. Under the trees my banger is waiting. So, you are indeed gone. I'm going to miss you. You and me, we go back a long way. We've 'ad some fun; you with the mic doing Karaoke what went on too long and you nearly pissing your pants! Laugh? I nearly pissed mine! We'll never have another evening of pints and chasers that always ended you with your hand up some girl's skirt. I'll always remember your dirty laugh that had people's heads turning in the street. But I won't miss having to meet you at the prison gates and you asking me for a loan 'to see you through'.

I am getting into the car; can see something tucked under the wiper! It's a sealed envelope. It's got my name on it. I open it...

> *'They tried to get me—but I 'got' me first!*
> *Hope this cheque sees you right mate.'*

> *Marty*

THE VICE PROVOST

I took an early train, to allow time to wander through the town. 'Maggie' in the local shop, more than welcoming. Intense interest in my reason for visiting so early. Nosey, in effect. I shouldn't have mentioned the interview.

'Well if you're going to be working for 'im, watch out for yourself. He's alone now, wife died three years ago... I'm not one to gossip but it's generally known 'is 'ands do wander; as do 'is thoughts, I'll bet. Mainly it's them littlest boys you know... 'e gives them afternoon tea Sundays...in the drawing room... no adults with them... the thought sickens... shouldn't be allowed! Poor little blighters. Know what I mean?'

Moving round the shelves I avoided contact. Advice came freely when I paid for my postcard.

'AND that Christmas panto... 'appens in that Morning-Room every year. New little boys write the script. It's re'earsed with 'im after lessons. Lower school boys and staff's the audience. 'e is always the "dame". Of course the little boys laugh at his wigs, silly songs, make-up and high-heels. But what do they know? Poor little innocents. Their first run-up to Christmas away from 'ome and family. We can only guess at what 'e's up to. I ask you ... with all this bother in the newspapers. Can't be long before 'e's caught ... watch your own back though, I say.'

≈

Access to his Georgian house was through trellis, well pruned roses and lavender. A polished brass plaque;

Vice Provost's House

My knock echoed inside. The Housekeeper opened, smiled, wet hands being dried on apron. A draught of ironing and cakes, polish and moth-balls.

The Vice Provost stepped forward. A courteous welcome. I recalled the deep folds of his smile and his proffered enormous hand, the prolonged handshake. His welcome was friendly, formal, but a little reticent.

'The Morning Room I think, as the day is so fair'.

He looked older than I had remembered from my interview; tall, stooped, lanky. In the past, a rower maybe? His suit; 'over-cooked-spinach' green, with thin lines of red and yellow, well-polished brogues, paisley cravat, yellow socks; corrugated to reveal white ankles.

I was shown to a settee. Elegant and spacious... perhaps this house's original furniture in view of its state of dilapidation. I sat... down almost onto the floor; my knees well above my waist. Would I ever get up, maintain a semblance of decorum and survive the lack of any back rest or support?

My interview a few weeks before had been in the Vice Provost's office; a strikingly business-like place. But now, exquisite china cups; pink roses and gold rims, tiny handles, scalloped edges... chipped. Drinking was a challenge. I commented on them, trying to divert my host from the dribbled coffee on my chin.

'The whole set belonged to my great Grandmother... wedding present from Disraeli I understand. Not that I've lived up to that lineage much.'

Deep in his throat a voice; plummy, aristocratic. Years of ecclesiastical sermons, three hundred tail coats ranked and listening.

The swaged, gracious room shouted, 'establishment, tradition and power!' He pulled up a button-back chair. Turkish rug ruched under rusted castors. He was too near! His intention, friendly though I think. His smile was again enveloped in deep folds of skin. Breath... cabbage. Fancy after-shave... Large hands offered biscuits. Immaculate nails with traces of red varnish, a monogrammed signet ring.

A brief meteorological chat ensued; awkward. He snapped into duty-mode. Offered a formal welcome to College and to my ghost-writing post.

'I recall at your interview that you said you wanted to leave teaching.'

'Yes. As you know, my husband died four years ago. I have been lonely in the city... difficult to make friends there... I tried but there was no community feeling. I was brought up in the countryside, a village, neighbours and friends nearby. I missed all that. So this is a new start; a different life.'

'Well, here there certainly is a community. It is a very long-standing one but like all such places there are those who gossip and have 'busy-body' tendencies. You will have to be discreet and tactful.'

'I have read your book. As I said at the interview your style is accessible and that is exactly what I want for my auto-biography. You are clearly very well read. I recall our conversation about Rider Haggard during the interview; his mannered style. Most people don't know who he is you know. Virginia Woolfe came up I think?'

'That's what I love about reading... the individuality of style to fit the purpose.' I said.

'How would you describe your "style" then? Not too young and modern I remember.'

'Mmm... I enjoy writing. I try to write in the style that's best for the subject. I am happy for you to guide me, to tell me what you want.'

He nodded, sat back with finger tips touching.

'You'd be working closely with me... but I would try not be too much of a "task-master".'

≈

A distant phone rang. He hauled himself up, apologising.

Time to scan the room. A clock ticked.

Spacious; threadbare; floral; softly-furnished. Grand floor-to-ceiling sash windows, through which the sun shone onto worn carpets.

I took the moment alone, to struggle out of the settee. Outside there was an abundant, well-tended, rose garden. A large pond with stone satyr holding up an urn to the sky as water trickled down his naked body to the pool beneath. Thick green algae grew on his lower limbs. Goldfish circled at his feet, nibbling aggressively at his toes.

Beside a chair, books, a pair of red 'Hockney' spectacles, some nail varnish... also bright red.

Photos of uniformed boys in rows were ranged on the mantle-piece. Central were two striking images, larger than the rest and black and white. The young Vice Provost in smart cricket-whites leaned over a smiling young woman who was seated; her hair neatly plaited and coiled over her ears. His hand rested on her shoulder. She smiled up into his face. The other, a boy in cricket whites, held a bat; alone, proud, serious. I recognized him. I had passed him in the hall... a large oil painting... in a monstrous gold frame.

The village-shop's gossip rustled around me.

I leaned over the pot-potpourri on the table... lavender, cloves, dried orange peel and rose petals; ancient and homely smells.

≈

He returned.

'Love the perfume of that stuff,' he said, 'takes me back to ...' paused, 'happier times you know... now where were we? Oh Yes... come and sit here by my desk.'

He pulled up a wooden chair and we both sat beside the huge desk, our chairs turned towards each other but not too near.

'This certainly is a close community here. We have, in our hands, future generations of World Leaders, you know ... "Movers and Shakers"'.

He sat back, looked out of the window.

'Only little "nippers" when they start, but many will go on to positions of privilege and power in the world. We care for them, give them the background and security of a large and broad-minded family.'

He leant back in his chair, adopting a more confidential tone.

'We are going to have to get along together when term ends next week. We'll be working closely as you know. These memoirs of mine... I hope they'll give me a "purpose" in my retirement.'

He stopped and looked at his hands.

'You understand that I must be able to trust you. Personal secrets... innermost thoughts... and so on?'

Leaning forward he spoke more quietly.

'You said at your interview, you were good at keeping secrets. You will have to be. Close-knit round here you know... word gets around... gossip abounds.'

He reached in his top pocket for the spectacles, shook out his freshly ironed handkerchief to polish the lenses. His unfocussed eyes seem older than he was.

'Recently there has been a lot of it...' he held up the lenses to the light '...of a very personal and degrading nature. Unfounded of course. I have to be sure of ... of your discretion.'

His spectacles now in place, he leant forward with an anxious look. Too close again... cabbage.

I nodded to reassure. We both smiled.

≈

As I left, I saw the oil painting again. The boy; probably eleven-years-old, in his formal school-uniform now. The Vice Provost saw me looking.

'Handsome young thing... I miss him so much... such a shock! Look at that aristocratic nose, his still-chubby cheeks. Striking eh?'

An awkward pause. He turned quickly to shake my hand.

'See you Monday morning at ten o'clock then. Hope you find the Cottage to your liking.'

'Yes', I said, 'I look forward to it and thank you for making me so welcome.'

≈

An enquiring look followed me round the village shop. I avoided it and bought a notebook and pen... in silence.

RECONCILIATION

He rested his weight against the desk behind him and read quietly from a small leather-bound book. His audience; Year-9 boys to whom Shakespeare was more likely to be the name of a pub than the Bard. As he read, a lump developed in my throat. I looked around. We were all silent. His voice was always quiet; now it was also emotional.

> *'Come gentle night; come, loving, black-brow'd night,*
> *Give me my Romeo; and, when he shall die,*
> *Take him and cut him out in little stars,*
> *And he will make the face of heaven so fine*
> *That all the world will be in love with night,*
> *And pay no worship to the garish sun.'*

He stopped... continued to look at the page... completely still.

The end of the lesson bell rang. Without looking up, he lifted his hand to dismiss the class.

After-school rumours were that Mr. W. Sawbey, middle-aged Head of English, had broken down in class. Those who had witnessed this emotional moment reported that a tear or two had slipped down the side of his large nose. Others described an utter breakdown of control, sobs that required a pause in his reading, a fumbling for handkerchief, a blowing of the great nose.

He lived in our road. After school I stamped down brambles along the path behind the houses. Who was his Juliet? What was his story? I ducked under overhanging hawthorns. The fence was broken down. His house and garden were in deep shadow, shrubs grew around the bay window. I crouched in the dusk; waiting, listening, edging closer. There were voices inside. The curtain was not fully closed, it was a warm evening and the window was ajar.

Mr. Sawbey was standing beside an old lady in a wheelchair. He had brought her tea. Her face was a mask; inanimate, exaggerated wrinkles, aged skin. He stooped to kiss her cheek. They talked and laughed. So... NOT his Juliet... his mother.

I could see in clearly without being seen. Her chair was surrounded with tables, radio, TV remote, tape recorder and cartons of drink. There were flowers by the window. I walked home.

Mum was going to be late. I made myself a sandwich, watched TV until it was dark, did some homework. It was boredom that made me creep back along the hedge.

A woman was folding clothes by the bed. She stooped to take Mrs. Sawbey's hand and say something into her ear.

'Annie, you are such a kind help to me. Before you go could you open the window a bit more, it is going to be long hot night I think.'

I ducked as Annie came to open the window a little.

Mr. Sawbey came in with a tray.

'How about a drink to cheer you up Mother?'

'Good idea, thank you Darling.'

'Not just water tonight I guess, the 'real thing' eh?'

'Yes please but I expect you've marking to do. So off you go. I'll listen to the radio for a while. Thank you William. I wish I wasn't such a nuisance.'

'It's just how life is Mother, you looked after me; now it's my turn to do the same for you.'

'Goodnight Darling...'.

Her voice was husky and very quiet... almost a whisper.

I bunked off school the next day. Mum left for work. I lay on my bed listening to music. My timetable was dull on Tuesdays. After half an hour I began to think about Mr. Sawbey. He would be impressed if I'd re-read the whole play. I turned to my copy of Romeo and Juliet. I had never read it like that, only in scenes and excerpts, but well before the fight and Tybalt's death my mind wandered to thinking of Mrs. Sawbey. What kind of a life had she had? What must it be like to be so old and disabled?

I crept back to the house. The curtains were open so I watched again, without being seen.

She sat for a long time gazing at her lap. Very still. Silent. Her lips moved as if she was whispering... praying maybe? Eventually rallying herself, she wiped her eyes and searched the table beside her. Her old fingers felt the water jug, TV controls; it was clear that she had poor sight. With gentle pats she reached past the radio. She reached out further past a small glass vase with a rose in it. Finally with a shift of her position in the chair she lunged in an effort to feel for the far side of the table. Her weight on the table tilted it to one side suddenly. She, her chair and the table with its contents tipped over with a crash. She cried out as she tumbled onto the floor.

Without thinking I climbed quickly onto the windowsill, I opened the window and jumped into her room. A smell of lavender soap and disinfectant struck me as I picked up the table. I explained that I was just passing and I knew her son, Mr. Sawbey, from school. She was very light when I helped her to sit up on the floor. She clung onto me. 'It's very kind.'

She had fallen beside her wheelchair. With her arms round my neck, it was easy to lift her into it. Her breath was short, she kept trying to speak, to say sorry. She sat in silence with her old hands clutching each other, her lips muttering. After a few minutes she said,

'How wonderful that you were passing just then. Thank you. Thank you.'

I moved the table close to her chair and replaced her things, then pulled up a chair to sit beside her.

'Shall I get you a cup of tea?'

'Just a new jug of water please?'

When I returned, she took my hand. I pulled up a stool so I could hear her soft voice.

'How the mighty have fallen eh? You never think, when you are young, that life could end in this slow, pointless way. I've had such an interesting and useful life, you know. Used to be a code-breaker in the War. We were buried in concrete rooms, could feel the bombs dropping nearby?'

Her eyes were wet as she talked. She watched my face closely to read my reactions. Eventually she sighed and said she was very tired.

I asked if I could get her anything. She repeated her thanks and said she would be sure to tell her son how kind I had been.

'That's nice of you Mrs. Sawbey,' I said, 'but... well... I am meant to be ill. That's why I am not at school. If you tell him I was here I'll be in all sorts of trouble, so please just keep it a secret. It was lucky I was nearby and could help.'

She smiled and understood.

'There's just one thing you could do for me dear, before you go', she said.

'Could you take me into the bathroom?'

She took a small yellow container from beside the sink. I pushed her back to her room, set her up near her table again. She held my hand. She was trembling from shock and very cold. I tucked a blanket on her lap.

'You'll never know how grateful I am for your help Dear. These pills are so important to me.'

I climbed back out of the window; at once, intruder and saviour.

≈

Later that day I saw Mr. Sawbey walking home. I hoped that his mother would keep her promise. A few minutes later an ambulance arrived. I watched them carrying out a stretcher. They had pulled the blanket over her face.

The Police who came to our door asked if we'd seen anything. Mum told them we'd both been out all day. I cringed at the thought of them checking the school registers.

The local paper reported: 'Local teacher Mr. W. Sawbey returned home to find his 90-year-old mother slumped in her wheelchair. An ambulance arrived within minutes but it was too late. The autopsy found that she had taken her own life.'

≈

Three years later, back in England from my Gap Year in Africa, I contacted Mr. Sawbey. He was surprised to hear from me but seemed happy enough to meet for a coffee. I still carried a weight of guilt about the part I'd played in her death.

As I walked to meet him I thought about the people in South Africa's 'Truth and Reconciliation'. The brutal offenders who had to confess to murder, rape and abuse, to those who had suffered at their hands. Truth and reconciliation? Was either really possible when the death of a loved one was involved? Did they ever really feel reconciled? I certainly couldn't.

He gave me an enquiring look after we had ordered coffee.

'I want to tell you something Sir.'

'My name is William. I am no longer your teacher, remember!' He laughed.

'This is going to be difficult for me to say... difficult for you to hear.'

He sat very still, eyes fixed on my face.

'I know that in some way... inadvertently... I was responsible for your mother's death.'

'You were?' he said.

'I knew how it happened, but I was scared to tell anyone.'

He stared into my face, put his cup down.

I could think of nothing to say. He leaned forward across the table. He pushed his saucer to one side and stared at me.

'Go on.'

I told him the full account of that day.

He looked at his lap when I finished. A long silence developed. He shook his head slowly.

'If you knew how it happened, why didn't you tell the Police? Why didn't you talk to them about it at the time? Why leave it till now, three years later?'

I could think of nothing to say. I had, in effect broken into his house that day.

'All right,' he said, but I can see the best course of action is for me to tell you my side of the story. Trust you with it.' He spoke quietly across the table.

'Mother had had a very bad time, the night before. I sat with her to the small hours. She talked... her interesting life... how lucky she'd been, how she knew she had helped to win the War, but how her quality of life was now.... pointless and painful. She didn't usually grumble... probably didn't want to worry me. I sat by her bed listening. Her frustration; having to sit in her room all day, not being able to do anything independently, to have no control over anything... every minute of every day. I mentioned the Day Centre and she began to shout and protest through her tears.

By the time it grew light outside we had been over and over the possibilities of Residential Homes, a live-in Carer, people who might be able to visit her... all kinds of ideas; every one of which made me feel guilty, and her angry. She returned always to the fact that she wanted to have the right to die by her own hand. She didn't want to implicate me; neither did she want me to feel badly. She reassured me constantly... I'd done all I possibly could but she knew she wanted to die with dignity and not to suffer her present life any longer. She knew how to do it but she wasn't physically able to carry it out... she was a strong woman, used to making her own decisions; being in control.'

His voice had become strained, quiet. He sat back in his chair.

'Let's go for a walk. It would be easier to tell you my full story; to trust you with it.'

We walked in silence to the canal, joined the tow path, and then, without warning, Mr. Sawbey began to talk.

'I wavered between thinking that I should give up my post at school or use up our savings to have someone to live-in. That evening I went to my room and lay on the bed. The situation, a philosophical, moral dilemma that I could envisage for myself sometime in the future. In that position I knew I'd feel the same. I must have dropped off to sleep. But as I woke up with my alarm ringing, I knew what I wanted to do. I just had to admit that I couldn't help her. I lacked the courage to give her what she longed for... control over her own destiny... or did I?'

He looked anxiously at me.

'So what did you do?

'When I was dressed and ready for work I went into her room. I gave her breakfast with a rose from the garden on the tray. I packed my briefcase and just before I left for work I went back and without her seeing. I put her sleeping tablets on her tray. My decision overnight seemed such a betrayal of someone who had cared for me all my life. It was time I was strong and gave her what she wanted above all things.'

With a slight contortion of his face he took out his

handkerchief and blew his nose, fumbling, taking his time.

'I had a difficult day at work... unable to concentrate or focus. Walking home that evening was terrible. I knew what I had done.'

He stopped. His expression hardened and he looked straight into my face.

'There was an autopsy afterwards because she had not been seen for a while by a doctor' he said. 'It was a stressful time for me, standing up in the Coroner's Court. Annie said she had tidied Mother's room about 10.00 am. She had found the room in some chaos, with things on the floor and in the wrong places. Mother seemed unaware of the muddle and was brighter than usual. Annie described how she had tidied away all the things on the tables and set the whole room straight. When questioned about the tablets she explained that she didn't remember exactly whether she saw the sleeping pills, but that she was always careful to put all tablets out of reach of her patients.

The Coroner concluded that my mother must have had access to the tablets somehow, perhaps she had taken a handful of them at some time and hidden them in preparation for her action. The Court's decision was 'misadventure'.

We walked in silence for a few minutes.

'So, thank you James,' he sighed and frowned, 'I feel that I can put it all behind me now I know the facts. I hope you can too.'

I nodded. He slowed his pace, stopped and looked into my eyes.

>'A glooming peace this evening with it brings;
>The sun tomorrow will not show its head:
>Go hence with no more talk of these sad things:
>We shall be pardon'd, and not punishéd.'

'Shakespeare will forgive me for misquoting just this once I think,' he said smiling.

(Misquotes from 'Romeo and Juliet' by William Shakespeare.)

SPECIAL EFFECTS

In the dark, wet espadrilles ooze, hissing at each step. Pushing through the trees that overhang the water by the boathouse, trailing branches brush my face. I untie the rope; the iron ring clinks. Ripples tap and splutter. Rowlocks creak. The boat moves out into open water. I am an integral part of its black surface; an aquatic bug, legs dipping and slashing. The night is still. Moonlight creeps behind strands of cloud. In the shallows, by the island, I rest in the pitch black. The moon is clearing distant trees.

I can almost feel him here beside me again; warm, breathing; near. A shared silence.

The rocks beneath are dark. I know them, stranded with weeds; delicate strings that waft with the movement of the boat, weaving and shifting, graceful and calm.

I whisper; my throat constricted with grief;

> 'My true-love hath my heart, and I have his,
> By just exchange one for the other given.
> He loves my heart for once it was his own,
> I cherish his because in me it bides.'

His life in the High Court was to seek honesty and justice. He had his personal touch, listening, understanding; dogged in his fight for truth.

His loss was felt by many. But my grief was the greatest.

≈

His personal 'effects' had to go. I face them bravely, alone. The rails and shelves above are now empty. His shoes; the most upsetting. They had been out for walks, polished for church, buffed on the days at work. His flowery yellow plimsolls are waiting, in a box, for the grandchildren's Christmas laughter. These shoes hold the most potent memories; poignant, intense, overwhelming. I kneel on the floor in his dressing room. I see them, ballroom dancing; on a tennis court; lying, kicked off in front of the fire; leaking sand from the beach and running up the front steps at the end of a day.

My sniffing echoes round empty rails and shelves. Where are his monogrammed handkerchiefs when I need one?

≈

I think the harrowing job is complete, but the mop touches something under the shelf. A small leather suitcase. I've never seen it before. No airport tags, labels or stickers. Strangely, it is locked. I sit on the bed to force open the lid.

Had he picked up someone else's case at the airport? Why didn't he tell me or try to give it back? I lift each item out, placing them beside me on the bed. There is a perfume. French. Expensive.

An elegant black pencil-skirt. A lavender blouse, pleated bib and black trimmings. Ah! They were like the old-fashioned uniform the maids used to wear. So this case was, perhaps, hidden by a maid and forgotten. But the black jacket with wide lapels was not an item of household uniform and on the lapel a broach is pinned; flat Celtic cords of silver that trace never-ending circles. I unpin it to look for the hallmark. A crown over a heart; Dublin, 1810. There is a tiny inscription: 'Love you forever'. Holding it in my palm, I know I have seen it before. His grandfather had given it to his grandmother on their wedding day. It was a story the old lady had loved to tell. Her eyes would well-up at memories of romance, love, intense happiness. He had knelt at her feet on the porch of their grand home, to give her the little box. I had not seen it since she had died. Would Piers have given this object of family love and romance away?

Had he given it to someone else? Had it been stolen?

I put it in my jewellery case. I would wear it on Friday at his memorial service in the Westminster Abbey. If Piers is watching me he'll know that I know.

≈

I crept again to the dark trees by the boathouse, seeking solace and privacy. In the shadows by the island I rest the oars. The suitcase and its contents have changed my weeping; into rage. Thinking back to the silk knickers I had found under the jacket; the suspender belt; fine seamed stockings and delicate hanky tucked into a lacy brassiere. At the bottom of the case, covered with a purple scarf, a pair of stilettos. As I closed the lid I saw a bulging zip pocket. Inside something soft flopped over my hand like a creature on the brink of death. A blonde wig.

Whose case was this? A stout German joining him at his Gilbert and Sullivan, a Suffragette-type who read Goethe, or a rather 'gone to seed' old trout he'd met at his London Club?

≈

Later when packing a firelighter into the case, I set a match to it. Smoke rises through the trees by the boathouse; a stink of betrayal, black and acrid; a sophisticated, perfumed, dead smell. It feels good, this fire. Flames lick round her clothes; soon she will be gone.

The case is beginning to catch fire. As the lid melts and crumples, I see a zip pocket splitting and curling in the heat. There is something white in it... an envelope. I snatch it out.

Through my tears I see photos. She's wearing clothes I recognize. I don't know her. In the last one, she has taken on an exaggerated pose; jaunty and smiling, head on one side, one pert finger under her chin.

There is no mistaking his wink.

'My true love hath my heart and I have his' from Elizabethan poet, Philip Sydney.

ROGATION DAY

The towering barn door swung open, hinges groaning an elephantine rumble that I felt in my chest. Scampering feet rustled in the straw. We waited.

A deadened stillness settled. Motes hung in the sunlight from the open door. Our shadows lay, black across the beaten earth before us. Cast in that dust was a history of wheels, hooves, boots and harvests. The same dust curled above the hay-loft, in the slipstream of the door's draught. Slowly the mice forgot that we had frightened them; they scuttled, well-hidden, about their business.

He stood behind me to whisper close in my ear.

'I wonder what thou, and I did, e're we lov'd, were we not weaned till then, but sucked on country pleasures, childishly.'

He put his arms round me. We stood a long moment. His body warm as I leant back against him. Silenced by the barn's sturdy grace.

'Look at this place,' he whispered. 'Is *this* a place for kissing?'

I felt his breath in my hair, warm and slow.

'Yes.'

I smiled up at him and loved him more than words could say.

He took me in his arms, sighed and stroked my forehead; bent to kiss me.

≈

Earlier in the day we had stopped at a small Norman church. Its walls plain white, the windows narrow and deep-set. In the chancel stood an elaborate Tudor tomb. A local family of landowners had marked their wealth and power in Tudor times. Their benevolence and rank chiselled into the stone.

He turned and held me at arm's length, looking deep into my eyes. I stepped away as he stooped to kiss me.

The sun shone through the angled squint that had allowed Commoners to see the altar. Two bell ropes hung in the tower, here were vestiges of a wall-painting, a row of family hatchments hung in the nave. The Norman font, the simple window in the north wall, white and undecorated. Certainly it was a Holy Place.

On a bench in the grave-yard, in a cool breeze, we looked at the ruined castle in the distance. Standing on a motte above the small town, it had protected the townsfolk for hundreds of years.

'It's all about our past; fighting, farming, surviving... a belief in an 'All Powerful God'. I said.

His head was bowed and he picked at a finger nail.

'Just now when I took you in my arms to kiss you...'

'We were in a sacred place in there.'

'Please don't tell me you are believer!' I shook my head. We sat apart and silent. A tractor was working nearby; seagulls squabbling behind it.

'Somehow it seemed... just wrong,' I said.' It was built as a place for worship; not for kissing.'

'So, does God not want us to love each other? That's his standout message isn't it? Loving.

'It just feels... disrespectful... sexy kissing in there.'

He brushed his hair off his forehead, took out his sunglasses; looked at the view.

' I thought you didn't believe in God.'

'I don't, but other people's beliefs should be respected.'

'So what is disrespectful about a loving kiss?'

He stood up and took a step forward, still gazing into the distance. I stood close beside him.

I took his hand and said,

'I just think this old church was built for the people of the parish; to come and worship God; not to kiss and fondle. That has no place here. For hundreds of years villagers will have come from the fields with their worries; to pray and seek peace. They believed in God, in His understanding and His presence. They'd have been brought up to think of it as a sacred place of refuge, they would have come here to hide from enemies, to sing His praises, share their thoughts and anxieties. It would have been a truly holy place to them; protecting and safe. The centre of their community... very precious. That's all.'

He walked ahead of me down the hill, head down and hands in pockets. I picked some flowers and ran after him. He took them, swinging them roughly as he strode on. Usually he pointed out the hedgerow flowers, comfrey that was added to cottage compost heaps for the nutrients in the leaves that was brought from deep in the earth by its long roots. Or purple ground-ivy under our feet that the Elizabethans used to perfume the hay on the floors of their houses.

~

Now, in the barn, he turned to me; took my hand. We walked beside each other under an ancient rhythm of solid oaks that strode overhead. Sturdy tie-beams supported three massive crown posts. Rafters spread like ribs under the tiles. The tooled flints in the walls, were set, like teeth in the security of their mortar. Putlog holes punctuated the flint and stone. Hanging swags of cobwebs puffed and wafted in ventilation slits.

'Well,' he said looking up at the highest beams, 'this is my church, my place of peacefulness and calm.'

There was that smile again. He took me in his arms, to kiss me, then stepped away and walked further into the barn. Above us, on the middle beam were hooks and the long ropes of an old swing.

'Come on then,' he called.

He stood behind me on the seat. Its trajectory; slow, long and majestic. Together we made the air race past us, faster and faster.

'I want to shout and sing.' I called over my shoulder.

He tipped his head back and sang up to the rafters. His strong voice, rough and untrained.

> *'Come my Lass and let's be jolly,*
> *Drive away dull melancholy,*
> *For to grieve it is a folly,*
> *When we meet together.'*

I joined in. It was a song he had taught me.

> *'Let union be, with all its fun,*
> *And we will join our hearts in one.*
> *I will go through as we begun,*
> *Since it is a holiday.'*

We sang it again and again. Slowly its force faded and our singing with it.

Beside us was an enclosure where wooden pegs were fixed in rows, the panels beneath them bruised into the shapes of the tools and halters that had hung there for centuries. He felt behind them, along the rough timber shelf, looking for the key to the hay-loft, but when we looked up, its door stood open above us.

The long polished stiles of the ladder had been darkened by many hands, the old beech rungs were faded with age, but still sturdy. As we climbed, the air was stuffy; hay, soil, rope, dust, diesel and animals. The window shutter was hard to open but once unbolted it swung out onto the sky and fresh air. Bending to see through the old frame, we saw the distant Downs, the river curving through coloured fields of Spring crops.

He sank into the hay with a deep sigh of contentment. There was a silence, seclusion; all sounds from below quiet and muffled. He pulled me gently down beside him. The air was dry and warm. My head rested on his outstretched arm. Rows of deserted swallow's nests nestled under the rafters. A long silence developed between us. The hayloft held us almost as meditation does; in silence, entirely still.

I knew he had kept many secrets from me. He would tell me nothing of his background or his life before we met in Oxford.

He sat up abruptly; pulled a long straw from the bale beside him. His hands were shaking as he wound it round his finger.

'This is the first time I have been back here since leaving school.'

He gazed across the repetition of ancient oaks, to their distant arching pattern.

'I've wanted to bring you here, ever since we met. It was a place of safety for me, away from home, along the footpaths and fields. Now I am here I get the same feeling of security.'

He turned to look down at me. 'I'd like to tell you. It has been hard to talk … but here, with you, it is OK.' He smiled and turned back to watch the dust curling in the draft of the open shutter.

'Ted Barker owns this barn, his tractor is parked in the yard. He still stores his hay and straw here. He made the swing for me, would bring snacks and water after school sometimes. Often I didn't want to go home. He hasn't taken the swing down. Maybe he guessed I would come back someday.'

I noticed that the straw he had picked up was now so tightly wrapped and twisted, it was stopping the blood from reaching the tip of his finger. I took his hand in mine to release it. He lifted his head to look into my face. A long gaze; his eyes filling with tears. We lay back into the hay.

'That's in the past' I whisper. 'We are the present. Our love has grown slowly into something wonderful. You have shared this place with me. I love it too. There is no going back.'

I touched his hands, his face, his lips. Tension faded. We lay together entwined and naked, making love gently before we fell asleep in each other's arms.

Barging and battering into the loft, a pigeon woke us with its panic and blunder, then it found the open window and flapped off into the April sky. Thin grey clouds streaked the palest of blues. It became a tiny dot and was gone. We lay close; his breath gentle and warm.

Far away there was the sound of music. He hummed the tune quietly.

'Must be Rogation Day' he said, 'processions, singing to thank God for farms, crops, animals. All of God's creation. So glad I no longer have to take part.'

His humming vibrated through me. The music stopped.

The barn door grumbled on its hinges. We ducked lower into the hay giggling. Footsteps and shuffling were below us, someone coughed. A male voice prayed; sonorous and loud.

> *'Let the earth bless the Lord: Yea let it praise him and*
> *magnify him forever.*
> *Ye fields and streams, bless the Lord:*
> *All green things upon the earth, Bless ye the Lord:*

He leant forward and covered me with his jacket. We hardly dared to breathe. We laughed silently. With his finger to his lips he turned away.

A voice rose from the foot of the hayloft ladder and began again.

> *'Almighty God, who has blessed us with this earth that bears*
> *fruits; bless the labours of those who toil in this barn. Bless the fertile*
> *crops here stored and treasured beasts in the byre.'*

A fiddle established a note, a tambour set a quiet beat and voices below joined in a hearty hymn. The great door rumbled open, feet shuffled. Slowly the singing moved away, down the track, out into the fields by the river.

I rolled over, bursting with giggles but when he turned to me, he was not laughing.

He sat up and frowned.

'This place is not for them. How dare they!' He beat the hay beside him with his fist.

'What are they doing here? It is a place of hard work, love, robust survival, sometimes even a refuge... nothing to do with God!'

I tried to take his hand but he pulled it away.

'For us it's about human trust and tenderness, as it has been for lovers for centuries. We are not kidding ourselves, like they are with their infantile beliefs. They have a right to do all that praying and singing in a church, but not here? No!

He stood up and began to pull on his clothes. 'That hocus-pocus here... in this true and hearty barn... disrespectful!'

I smiled and thought of the little white church that morning.

'Come on', I said. I'm hungry! Where's the nearest pub?

'I wonder what thou, and I did, e're we lov'd, were we not weaned till then, but sucked on country pleasures, childishly.' From 'Good Morrow' by John Donne.

'Come My Lass and Let's Be Jolly'. From Rev Baring Gould's collection of West Country Songs.

'FIVE, SIX, PICK-UP STICKS!'

Do you know that game Pick-up-sticks? We played it in the evening after Granny's funeral. You hold lots of thin painted sticks upright in a bundle on the table and then let them go ... clacketty-racket. They tumble into a heap. You take it in turns to get a stick out without moving any others. You get points for different colours; so best is the blue, there's only a few of them so they score highest points; greens are next highest score, then reds, and yellows are lowest. There are lots of them.

After the visitors had gone Mum, Dad, Giles and me, we played it in the kitchen. It was warm, smelled of cakes and wine ... and old people. Dad's hands were shaky, we laughed at him, but I was sorry we did that. Mum was usually slow but that night she rushed her turns without thinking. Giles was too little but he liked trying, so we let him keep a stick even when he shouldn't have got one. I was no good from the start. It was winding me up.

You know those dreams that stay with you, even when you wake up? That night I had one of those. Granny had died and when we played Pick-a-Stick at the table in the kitchen, I dreamed that I was God. You know God? The one who decides when people die or are born, get sick or commit murder. How does he decide though? It must be hard for him. Does he have a reason for choosing one person or another; a plan?

Well in my dream I was God. I looked down at all the people I knew and had to decide who would die next. Before I decided I kept thinking, I was so sorry Granny had been picked.

I wouldn't have chosen her. Everyone in our family felt like I did. Our lives all shifted somehow, once she had been taken away, just like the sticks. We would never be in the same place again. Nothing would be as good without her... and there I was, in my dream, kind of playing the same game ... being God. If I was going to be a good God, and loving, I should be picking people who could be taken off the pile without upsetting the others. I didn't want people to feel as bad as I did about Granny going.

Picking her up in the game would have been good, she would have given me a high score. She was a rare one. But I was God Almighty. I didn't need to score points. 'All mighty' must mean a 'top score' for God whatever happens. So I tried to get into God's brain. Why did he pick Granny? He must have known that she would be touching so many people in the pile. Were his hands sweaty or shaking or was he just not concentrating.

The thing about bad dreams is that they can go on, like another part in a serial. My dream about being God went like that the next night.

I looked down at Mum. If I took her, just think how it would be; we would all shift and fall. I remembered Dad, as he turned round to leave the church at Granny's funeral, his face twisted up like Giles when he was a baby. It would be much much worse if he lost Mum. And then what about Giles, he's only five. ... and ME? What if Dad was taken? I'd never even imagined that, but Dad would have to go sometime before the game ended.

≈

Playing Pick-up sticks, I looked at them, each one shifting the others as another was taken away without a reason. Maybe God jumbles us all up, closes his eyes and just takes the next person his hand touches.

Then I noticed the ones that fell away from the rest. I used to go for them if I got the chance; it didn't matter if my hands were clumsy. They were easy to pick up. Nothing touched them. They didn't move other sticks at all. Who were they in my dream? Maybe they were like the man who sits on the steps of the train bridge. He's got a smelly dog, a sleeping bag and a tin for you to put money in. I thought maybe he was one of those who wouldn't be missed. Could he be taken away without changing other people's lives? But then I thought of his dog. Who would care for him? He would miss the touch of his master, could die of hunger. And what about the people who give money? When they drop their coins into his tin, he nods. I guess there's something they like about helping him. They'd miss him a bit.

When I was God there was a stupid rhyme in my head

'One two buckle my shoe,
Three four knock at the door,
Five, six pick-up sticks,
Seven eight lay them straight,
Nine ten a big fat hen.'

So maybe there is no plan... no point... all random.

I've known those words since I was at nursery. Why did they teach me that? Did it teach me that there was no reason or answer? Who was the winner of the game, the hen who was knocking? Was the Almighty singing or playing? Was it me that was picking up sticks? What if it was me who laid them all straight, before a fat chicken? And who gave her buckled shoes on her feet? I was so little when I was taught to chant that rhyme. Was it meant to be helping me to understand the world?

Have you ever cried in your sleep? Well I did when I was God ... playing Pick-a-Stick Alone and All-mighty.

SPRINGS

Cautiously... onto the bottom step... small, bare toes splayed on the hall tiles... a glance behind him at the sitting-room door... slow movements of right hand onto bannister... one foot onto first step... intense controlled motion... his weight transfers... the greatest of care.

Stop! Listen! Look back at kitchen door.

Some stairs squeak... he knows them... he has removed his socks and stuffed them into his pockets...one hand grips the bannister... the other spreads wide against the wall beside him... fingers splayed... bitten nails digging into flesh under pressure... weight transfers from the hall floor... he is stealth... causing no sound. The next stride... onto the centre of the step... a gentle pull on the bannister for support... small toes impress the pile leaving light foot-dents behind him... tongue between his lips... a frown of concentration... each movement guided by an experiential map... his concentration searching ahead.

Shying away from creaks and groans... he picks his way with care... the judgement of seven years' experience. Progress is laboured... an act of exaggerated mime... completely silent.

Two steps from the top he releases his hold on the bannister... places his hands onto the very edge of the carpeted step ahead. Here is danger. For seven years he has developed his skills here.

Crablike he approaches on all-fours... left hand and foot on the centre of the stair-carpet ahead... right hand holding the base of the bannister... only one step remains. He pauses...this last step... the most dreaded of all perhaps the noisiest... he can make it... he pulls his thin body up... lifts his right foot onto the top step and unfolds to standing.

From the top of the stairs, he glances back at the closed sitting room door. It is still shut. The shouting has stopped.

The landing floor-boards are painted white. He had helped to paint them, down on his knees; with Gran supervising from a stool. They both liked the whiteness. She paid him some money for working hard; said he had been a 'Trooper'. 'A lovely job' she had said.

Later they laid the carpet-runner over those boards, he thought it a mistake. He had taken such care. Now he is grateful for that carpet, it muffles sounds as he tiptoes to the room at the end. Bending over the handle he turns it carefully with both hands. Stale air pushes past him as he opens Gran's door.

Immediately he is down into a soldiers' crawl, onto dusty floorboards under her bed. He ducks the angle-irons of the bedframe, wriggles to the centre. He rests his forehead on the backs of his hands. Sighs. Tries to imagine Gran lying above him, asleep. A tiny whorl of dust tickles his nose. He gropes for his hanky to extinguish a sneeze; sighs, relaxes his shoulders and legs, shuts his eyes, ready to wait.

This feels safe... at least for a while... until 'they' calm down. But sometimes the rows last for ages; with *this* man, it's been six years. Mum will wonder where he is, sometime. This is the worst row there's been.

It is beginning to get dark. He turns to look across the floor-boards to the door... should have closed it. If only there had been a key... he could have locked it. But 'wait'... he should not be able to see the door. The bedcover is tucked up under the mattress, he must have hitched it up as he crawled underneath. Not safe! He could be visible to anyone coming in.

Must not be seen; not found, like last time. He turns onto his back to slide out, steps gingerly across the floor to shut the door;

tipstoes back, pulls the cover down to touch the floor, slides under the bed again, resting his head back onto a dusty blanket by the wall.

Well-hidden now, this is as good as hiding places go. *Must* not go to sleep. Got to be ready. What kind of trouble if HE finds him?

Above his face a striped braid fixes the springs, one sewn onto the next in neat lines. They are old springs, coiled egg-timers of wire, flexible and strong, top and bottom, thin and weak in the middle, like waists. Guards, rusted in serried ranks, shoulder to shoulder, working together. He traces the rhythm of their shapes with his eyes, but keeps losing count. So he starts again with his finger.

The springs link together on supportive duties to the mattress above. They are strong. The regular wires are tightly fixed onto the angle–iron frame. Each is dependent on another, without them all, every one of them, holding on tight... who knows what could happen if one of them collapsed. But in the centre the braid above has worn out; yellowing, thin, nearly collapsing from the wire cradle with Gran's imprint bulging. It sags and is ready to fall at any moment. If anything disturbed it, the length of the collapse could go right to the edge of the bed. If it did give out, he could be injured.

He thinks of Gran, tries to see her face before she was in a wheelchair; wishes that he had been allowed to take her for walks. When he was little she taught him to blow the pollen out of the flowers in the garden, but told him not to do it often as the bees needed it. The troubles downstairs didn't happen when she was here.

His fingers follow the pattern of the stronger springs. He smells rust. With one finger he wipes one of the springs and leaves a clean space in the dust. His licks his finger; it tastes of blood.

What if someone came in to lie above him? The structure could finally collapse? If he could get out without being seen he could run to Martin's house. His mum was always there; she'd helped him before.

The house is strangely quiet below.

He goes back to clearing the dust away from every spring. He sees the safe cradle of braid until it reaches the middle.

The dust settles around him. He thinks again of Granny... pretending she is there, resting; alive. Things have changed. She used to take him out when the rows began. This man forbids him to go out on his own. Often he hears his friends on the Recreation Ground across the road, after school.

He closes his eyes and waits... listening for sounds from the house. It is quiet. The shadows on the floorboards are fading.

He would wait for fifteen minutes. He'd listen while his watch clicked round; tiny steps of time. He could go down very slowly and quietly. If Mum was there, on her own he could get something to eat. He'd run down the back stairs to Martin's if he heard the heavy footsteps coming. There was a curtain over the back stairs door near him. He could see the faded green velvet of the curtain trailing on the floor. Maybe he could hide behind that if someone came. Then all he'd have to do is to open the door and run down the steps and out of the wash house.

Something moved in the angle–iron frame. A ladybird. How lucky is that? His favourite... a Two Spot; red with two black spots. This must be a lucky sign. He'd read about them. This one had found a good place to hide; a good dry place to last all winter.

He watched it settle into the corner-joint in the bed-frame; it shuffled about. Finally it drew in its legs and was still... asleep maybe... still ready for action if anything happened.

He listened again. There were quiet steps approaching the door. This must be Mum. Whatever *he* did was loudly done. But, just in case he curled up into his smallest. She knew where he'd be. He'd hidden here before.

She whispered his name. 'It's OK... safe to come out. He's gone... gone for good... gone for always.'

THE MORAL MAP

I passed a pleasant time that afternoon in bookshops, before walking to the station. I'd long been researching the life and times of Charles Booth who, from 1886 to 1903 created an early example of social mapping: 'Inquiry into Life and Labour in London'. By means of a colour coding system, street by street and region by region, the level of poverty and social class of the residents was recorded. Charles Booth had been an excellent subject for study in my youth. Now, in retirement I had the opportunity to read and research further into the morals of the Edwardian Metropolis. During a pleasant roam through the second-hand bookshops, I had found a more recent publication about Charles Booth entitled 'A Moral Map of Edwardian London' by Thomas Gibson. Jubilant that I had found it I considered it to have been a day of excellent good fortune.

I examined the cover's sepia portrait. Charles Booth, moralist and social scientist. I was as elated as a man of my years could ever be as I travelled home. In prospect for me was a wider knowledge and understanding of this remarkable man.

≈

In the train, I took the book out of its bag, rested it on my lap. For a long while I examined the sepia portrait of Booth, his distant look, pen in his right hand and folded wire spectacles in his left. The crumpled cloth map of London spread on the desk; some well-worn pocket notebooks by his side.

As the train pulled into its first stop and before the doors opened, a raucous crowd of schoolboys pressed against the windows. I could see passengers moving into the next compartment, the 'quiet carriage'. I thought momentarily, of joining them, but considering myself to be of a broader frame of mind and, having always enjoyed the company of generations other than my own, I stayed with my precious book and boisterous young companions.

~

They burst into the compartment, pushing and jostling. Their school-bags swinging and cumbersome. Conversation, limited by a narrow vocabulary was composed mainly of the 'f' word. I noted too that syntax, never a strong point of the young, was entirely absent. Single words, short phrases, grunts and raucous shouts; all at high volume. There was a rhythm, a frequency of the use of the 'c' word. 'Like' was scattered liberally offering no impact on meaning that I could discern. I looked for another adult in the compartment. There was none. I swiftly covered the parcel on my lap with my coat. School bags were aimed at heads, scuffed shoes jumped and climbed the seats. A fight developed by the door amongst the dropped litter.

The boy beside me turned and smiled.

'Would you like a sweet?' He held out fruit pastilles, 'These are my favourites.'

'That is really kind of you, thank you,' I replied and, by way of introducing more of a civilized social interaction, I asked, 'Which school do you boys attend?'

'St Peter's in Deacon Street.'

'Ah yes, used to be a Grammar I think.'

Their blazer pockets pictured a crest and the school's Latin motto. Interesting... it took me but a few moments to translate; 'Honour. Respect. Service'—good principles all, for the aspiring young. I turned to my book and my young companion, to his magazine.

'Here, what do you think of these?' he asked me, holding out a full-page colour photograph. 'Big aren't they? Do you like tits?'

Without, I hope, any sign of outrage I said,

'Well, they are certainly very big, but ...'

'But do you like them? Wouldn't you like to give them a squeeze?'

'I can't say I like or dislike them. To me it seems degrading for the young lady concerned.'

The boys sitting nearest to me had fallen silent during this exchange, but now they burst into shouted laughter.

'Degrading, degrading,' they chanted and fell on the magazine, tearing all the images of breasts out, displaying them on the seat opposite mine. When the train pulled into my station I walked speedily out of the train, taking no notice of the jeering boys inside.

≈

By the fire that evening, a port in my hand, I was gloomy. I turned to my new book. Charles Booth had devoted his life to the improvement of living conditions, education and morals of his age. It was his belief that the first step in achieving this aim was to know where there was such a need within the City. With this knowledge society could provide the necessary housing, health care and education for its citizens. In his day he wrote that every member of society had a moral responsibility to assist with this cause, in whatever way they could.

I gazed long into the fire and imagined how the Edwardians would have responded to those boys on the train. In our society, self-preservation and fear took priority it seemed. Citizens no longer felt duty bound to instil the higher moral values of the past. A pity! I rested my head against the antimacassar and as I drifted into sleep. I heard again the boy's voice, 'Do you like tits?'

And there they were, wafting and bouncing gently before my eyes; fulsome and enhanced in my dream by a black lace negligee.

I awoke with breasts on my mind. Not something that had happened to me for many a year.

But for all that... quite a pleasure.

THE WEST FAÇADE

The prevailing wind drives rain into the porch. The Tramp mumbles expletives; obscene, with reference to Christ, the 'Risen' Lord. He moves deeper inside. Steps of Gothic arches curve above his head; effigies of saints and disciples. Their praying stone hands and robes unmoved by the wind. By the huge doors the Tramp settles onto his cardboard. With laboured crossing of legs, he positions his tin in preparation for another day's supplication.

La Place de la Cathedral is silent. Empty.

The large doors are no longer closed during the day. More effort must be made to eliminate the off-putting dusty smell, cold damp air, wilted flowers. The Priest, influenced by the Mayor and Tourist Board, has had to recognize that 'footfall' takes priority; tickets, postcards and book sales. Income. The presence of a tramp at the entrance is an agenda item next meeting.

≈

From a third floor flat opposite, an elderly woman sits at her window. White against black, Claudette watches from her wheelchair. The cathedral's façade is powerful and gracious. Her rosary beads move in her hands as she watches.

Nothing. Except the Tramp and his dog.

The sky greens behind the Cathedral, presaging dawn. Two towers loom against the lighter grey in the East. Quite suddenly the sun glimmers in a transept window and the stone tracery turns black.

As if called to duty by the risen sun, the priest approaches, deliberate; briefcase in hand and cassock's hem flicking behind him on each step. He lifts the key chained to his waist, fumbles with the lock on the side entrance, enters. Moments later he heaves wide the huge west door. A gesture of welcome... is it? Inside it is cold and damp, but the morning air will freshen. An old woman shuffles past him to pray. He gives only a distant nod; looks over her head to the right and left. He hopes, perhaps, that today the Tramp will not come... but he is there on the steps beside him, with his dog, Gaston. He turns on his heels without a glance, genuflects to the east and strides into darkness.

The Tramp is cold in the ancient draught of lilies and incense from inside. Rubbing his hands he struggles to his feet and perches on a bench beside the steps. He tips his face to the early sun. Gaston, potters, sniffing round his morning route, watering the wheels of cars, tracing the scents of passers-by in the night. A woman, her wrap-around apron wet from the tap, has brought water to her window boxes. She flings it at the dog, shouting and menacing with her fist. Gaston laps her water from the gutter by her front door, whites of eyes showing as he watches her, prepared to flee if there's more abuse.

Past the finials and gargoyles of the southern buttress, the sun picks out details on the facade. Suddenly it clears the corner of the south wall, throwing into relief the stone lancets, the ordered mass of blank arcading, loggias, fluted columns, foliated tracery and canopies.

Josette arrives, with knitting and flask in a carpet-bag, a newspaper tucked under her arm. She stops to chat with the Tramp, hands him a white paper-bag; his breakfast it seems. He smiles and blows her a kiss as she unlocks her booth. Through the glass hatch inside she settles into her nest of tickets, books and postcards. Outside the Tramp attacks his breakfast. Bread is broken; an unholy cramming and munching. Quickly it is gone. No thought of Christ's flesh in his mind. But maybe he is missing the communion wine.

Claudette sees an artist setting up easel, umbrella and

paints. Taking care to choose the spot, she settles her stool onto the pavé. Her pencil outlines the facade's huge form with light confident sweeps.

The Tramp moves to the porch, the sun warms the pillars at his back. He and Gaston relax and wait; as motionless as the figures that rest in ranks over their heads. The Cathedral is immense. Lit now by the full morning sun it proclaims with grandeur the Christian belief in the Glory of God, the Father, Son and Holy Ghost. The righteousness of faith and teachings of Jesus Christ. *This* is the house of God. He reminds us of roles and responsibilities to Him, to Christ, to each other. He is all powerful. Obey. Be afraid.

Tourists come, sauntering in twos and threes. Claudette watches as they pass the Tramp's outstretched hand, glancing down at his biblical gesture. Few give as they enter. Inside the beseeching hands of the Madonnas that beg heavenward, remind them of their duty and more coins are given as they exit. No-one speaks to him; there is no recognition that he is a human with a need for bread or friendship. He takes from his coat a cardboard sign; 'pour manger s.v.p.', places it beside his tin.

Restaurants are opening their shutters. The tourists' stomachs are rumbling. They may remember that God will be watching. 'Give us this day our daily bread'? If they have bought into Christianity as their insurance policy for life everlasting, they will know that God must be logging all their actions. He, with the heavenly spread sheet before him, will certainly be keeping a daily record of their behaviour and generosity? Won't He? Few of them give though.

Two small boys swerve as they pass the Tramp, holding their noses and bursting with laughter along the street.

The local paper, open on the table beside Claudette, takes a formal slant on his situation. She leans forward to read.

'The Catholic Church cannot officially accept beggars outside their churches because, begging is officially forbidden by law in France, but they can turn a blind eye and often do so, in the spirit of charity.

Church funding is almost entirely for the "patrimoine", maintenance of the buildings, estates and art. There are many voluntary agencies throughout France to help support the Sans Domicile Fixe, more commonly referred to as SDF's. Hostels exist but they can be places of fear, with incidents of violence, theft and rape.'

The Tramp must find a safe doorway somewhere each night. But by arriving here early, he secures his place on the steps. Claudette reads another piece in the newspaper. It describes the threat that has been made by a radical group to the fabric of towns in the region. The headscarf has been banned from schools, colleges and streets. Unrest is stirring. The mayor writes with conviction that those who choose to live in France should be prepared to respect the ways and traditions of the French people. His is a courageous patriotic and popular stand.

The day warms the steps to the porch. The Cathedral becomes a flat faded backdrop. The carvings less striking. Humdrum. Drab.

A line of children approaches, their twittering punctuated by vigilant adults, barking as they shepherd. Small faces lift to peer up at the monolith against the blue above. Rules of conduct are repeated. Once quiet, they all move into the porch where Apostles are pointed out, notes are scribbled. A teacher steps back, upsetting the Tramp's tin, coins scatter and children stoop to collect and return them. The offending adult gives generously as recompense. Her gift is good. A note, into his hand; straight into his pocket with a nod but no smile.

Inside, Josette's treasures attract some pupils, others sit in the pews already tired. One girl turns as she enters the nave. With a guilty glance at her teacher, she runs back to the porch to give the Tramp a sweet, dropping it into his tin. He receives it with a nod; unimpressed. When the visit is over the children sit under the trees, rummage in their bags, quietening as they eat and drink. The Tramp sits watching them; an effigy of 'Blessed are the Poor'. Children drift across the square in pairs with clipboards, taking up positions on the benches, to settle and draw. Their faces hidden under sun-hats.

Concentration, calm and stillness settles. An earnest boy stays by the teacher talking. He points and she moves with him to a seat near the porch where he sits to draw the statues. But he seems to be looking more closely at the Tramp.

The cathedral absorbs the sun. The colours of the stone, bleach to a lighter grey. Heat, wavers in the air. Inside it will be cool. Claudette can recall how the colours from the chancel window will now be laid on the tiled pavement; a gothic network of lights through which it seems an honour to wade.

The children are gathered; counted. They shuffle away in a neat line of pairs, their chattering soon lost in the narrow streets. The Tramp moves with difficulty deeper into the shade of the porch and slumps into a doze. Josette locks up, leaving with her shopping bag. Gaston looks up as she passes, the end of his tail flips a greeting. An elderly couple hide in the shade to read their map. They bicker and point. There is tension. After their visit they stop in the doorway. She crosses herself, turns to look back. At the Tramp? No, he is again invisible, as is his tin.

The tawdry hush of midday heat settles. The cathedral absorbs and warms the dust in the air. The man in black arrives. Before he enters he glances up at the window where Claudette watches. Today he has a canvas bag over his shoulder, a musical instrument maybe. Maryse changes the flowers each day. She keeps a watch on him, doesn't like the way he looks at her legs as she climbs the ladder. The man in black sits behind a pillar in the darkest of the side-chapels. His routine is always the same. He has a plastic box in a shopping bag. He opens it. A surreptitious silent lunch is eaten with eyes lowered. There is a still secrecy that he shares with the radiance of the Madonna before him. Visitors whisper and pass; few see him in his corner. Those who do, assume he is devout. He is... to his lunch: he chews methodically and stays for exactly twenty minutes. Maryse thinks he is some kind of a pervert, a flasher even. She reports him regularly to the Priest.

'Do not judge that you may not be judged' he says.

Others have reported her for stealing the alter flowers from town gardens in the night. 'For the beautification of Our Father's House', she says when challenged, but cannot explain where her allocated funding for the flowers has gone. The Priest knows the truth but forgives her, 'In the name of the Father'. Flower-arrangers are hard to find.

Josette returns with market shopping bulging in her bag. She stops to exchange a few words with the Tramp, who peers into the small bag she hands him, looks up, smiles. He blows her a second kiss as she walks into the shade to unlock her booth. He watches her black shoes and plump white legs.

The Cathedral radiates the heat of the day. Its open doors offer a cool haven. The intricacies of the facade are now diminished, grey cardboard flattened, the full-frontal sunshine.

Clusters of students collect in La Place. A pageant of kissing and greeting takes place before they sit cross-legged on the flagstones and benches to smoke, compare notes, jokes and opinions. Tinny music, giggles and eau-de-toilette are in the air. Sometimes there is a shout of laughter, shrieks and name-calling. The artist shakes her head and begins on the north tower. Her paintbrush is busy on the palette before each stroke. Tourists sit on the steps that approach the porch. They share ice-creams and photos... for too long. The Tramp, leans forward and growls. He waves his hand to shoo them away from his tin. The students look round and mimic his disapproval to shouts of laughter.

An American in a ten-gallon hat speaks to the students. He then goes to the Tramp, offers sympathy and a friendly smile. The Tramp holds out both empty hands in return. 'J'ai faim, s'il vous plait, Monsieur, j'ai faim.' he mutters. The American turns to a passing student.

'What's he saying, this poor guy?'

'He says he is hungry, but a drink's probably what he really wants.'

'Oh gee that's easy.' He reaches for his shoulder bag and brings out a bottle of water, 'Here you go Buddy. It's my last bottle but I'd sure like you to have it. I can go buy some later.'

He strolls into the Cathedral. The Tramp swears and spits after him. The Stetson gleams from the nave.

A light breeze blows in from the pavement. Inside dust settles on marble heads, bowed in prayer. It forms thick cataracts on beseeching eyes, taints the colours of memorial shades and turns the old gold organ-pipes into brown plasticine.

At five o'clock, sad Hugues steps from his front door onto the side street. Time to walk his imaginary dog. He glances back at the long piece of black cloth trailing behind him, repeatedly checking that the 'animal' is following and behaving well. If, by chance, the 'beast' strays the wrong side of a post or snags against a grating, Hugues reprimands her.

> *'Laetitia! Sois gentille! Fais pas ça.'*

He ambles across La Place each evening, sometimes humming quietly to himself. Looking only at the pavement beneath his feet or back at Laetitia. The Tramp scowls as he watches his progress. When Hugues is near to the cathedral steps he shakes Gaston awake.

> *'Allez Gaston. La chienne. Va chercher la chienne.'*

Gaston struggles to his feet, shaking himself. Bounding and barking he sets off in search of his prey, but finding no dog to chase away, stops to sniff at the black cloth. A moment of drastic panic. 'Laetitia' is grabbed and crumpled into a tight embrace. Hugues stands very still, hunched and watching Gaston return to his master for a stroke and murmured praise. Hugues then walks with Laetitia safe in his arms, before setting her down again to continue on his way into the park. When he returns later he has already forgotten Gaston. He plods past the Tramp and his dog, who are both sleeping.

As the sun sets, shadows of the building opposite, begin their evening climb up the facade of the Cathedral. Darkness creeps over the doors and across the pointed fluting above the porch.

Graphite greys colour-in the Gothic, leaving only the shadow-silhouettes of the roofs of the houses opposite. Josette locks her booth, pauses for a few words with the Tramp, strokes Gaston and sets off for home. Gaston climbs onto the Tramp's lap where he seeks approval with a licking of hands. He is welcomed with murmured intimacies and stroking.

The priest closes and locks the doors. His stride is less determined. Somewhat stooped now he walks home to his flat in the Chapterhouse. A religious automaton but still respected by the community.

Suddenly a gang of youths arrive on motorbikes, revving and shouting to each other over their engines' roar. Then, with ignitions turned off, they unpack saddlebags of tins and bottles. They settle on benches to smoke and drink. They are loud, coarse; soon inebriated. One relieves himself against a tree, another later, into a litter bin. Gaston gets up quietly. He creeps behind the Tramp to hide. The shouting begins again, a row has broken out. La Place rings and rumbles with threats and abuse. The Tramp struggles to his feet, begins to move away quietly with Gaston at his heels, but a youth sees him, runs across to block his way, shouting and cursing, lifting his fists to the Tramp's face. Too much for Gaston. He leaps at the ankles below the raised arms. His growling is muffled by the trouser-leg clenched between his teeth. He dances, dodging under the attacker's feet, nipping and barking in a frenzy of courage. The Tramp's face is fear and rage, but knowing his own strength, he backs away to make a shuffling escape into a side street. Gaston must fend for himself.

A badly tuned guitar gives a rhythm, to which the young men cavort and leap. Running across benches and swinging on branches of the pollard planes. They whip each other into a substance-induced, primitive stamping. More join them to drum on the waste bins that have been left for early morning collection. The sun has now gone entirely from the scene, the Cathedral is slowly bathed in orange flood-lights. The gaudy, unholy colour they give to the stone is a Disneyland backcloth; eerie, theatrical and slowly too bright.

The 'tribal' dancing below reaches a climax that cannot be contained. They brawl; factions trapping and fighting in every corner. The noise of their fury, or maybe a phone call from one of the neighbours, eventually brings a siren into earshot. But before the Gendarmes arrive the bikers are gone, leaving behind them the debris and mess of their evening.

When La Place is empty, there comes again the slow shuffle of the Tramp. He approaches the doorway with Gaston at his heels. He had escaped from injury but forgotten his tin, to which he returns with relief. Then he searches out and drain the tins and bottles, quenching their thirst to help them through the night. In the darkness the gaudy floodlights abuse the beauty of the Cathedral. At eleven o'clock they are switched off.

Now the cathedral is barely visible. This is the moment when Claudette usually leaves her chair by the window, but tonight she stays. Globe-lights round La Place cast a subdued light. The day has been long for her. She is tired, but she waits for the moon to rise. She recalls the events of this day, full of human behaviour... only a soupçon of it humane or Christian.

She leans forward to watch four figures creeping along the shadows in the narrow road beside the cathedral. Their rucksacks bulky and balaclavas black. She turns out the light beside her. They crouch with shoulder bags in the porch. Conspiratorial glances over shoulders scan La Place. It is silent and dark.

ACKNOWLEDGEMENTS

Many thanks to...

Ruth Dowley, for her inspiring teaching and encouragement.

Sarah Watkinson for her gentle nagging and friendship.

Zoe Gilbert for believing in me.

Belinda Hough Robbins, Caroline Lawrence, Cathy Lawson and Trevor Smith—all reliable patient and honest readers.

Tessa Powell for the cover drawing and Jaine McCormack for introduced me to Tessa.

John Ballam for keeping me on track.

James Harrison for his publishing advice and expertise.